THE UNDERTAKER:
BLACK AS DEATH

D1612532

THE UNDERTAKER:
BLACK AS DEATH

George G. Gilman

NEW ENGLISH LIBRARY/TIMES MIRROR

NEL Books are published by
New English Library Limited,
Barnard's Inn, Holborn,
London EC1N 2JR.

Made and printed in Great Britain by
Hunt Barnard Printing Ltd,
Aylesbury, Bucks.

0 450 05157 9

For:
David Alan Coe —
if you ain't country,
so will I !

PROLOGUE

DURING the afternoon of an extremely hot day in the August of 1859, a boy of ten years old sat on a wooden bench in Battery Park at the very tip of Manhattan Island, a large book open on his knees.

For most of the time he read the book with intense concentration – studying the pages carefully and turning over the leaves with eager speed, voraciously seeking the endings to the sentences which were incomplete at the foot of each.

But occasionally he would look up from the book, to gaze out across the harbour of New York City.

He was a slightly built youngster, a little too thin for his height. More than adequately dressed for the heat of the day which was cooled not at all by the slight breeze which came in off the harbour. As is often the case with a boy of his age, he had started to outgrow the knickerbocker suit, shirt and cap which had fitted him not long ago.

On the occasions when he looked up from the book, the concentration he applied to his reading no longer showed on his pale face. Instead he wore an expression that was almost vacant – the kind of look a boy of his age might show if he were confined to a classroom, enduring a dull school lesson, and was able to sneak a glance out of the window at the sunlit yard where his friends were playing.

And although he was not in school on this humid Saturday afternoon, the boy did experience a feeling of being trapped. Enclosed by the trees of the park, the teeming streets of the city behind, the Hudson and East Rivers to either side and the busy expanse of New York Harbour in front of him. From which he could escape in spirit by reading the book or daydreaming when he abandoned the printed page to visualise in his mind's eye the images which were conjured up by the writer's descriptions. Images which, the book informed him, were there to be seen in reality at the other side of the ocean that stretched out beyond the harbour.

Anybody who knew the boy would have found nothing strange in his choice of a Saturday afternoon pursuit; for all who knew him considered him something of an oddity in everything he did.

But the elderly lady who paused in front of the bench during one of his preoccupied stares out towards the Narrows did not know him.

'A penny for your thoughts, young man,' she said in an amused tone.

He looked up, startled. 'I'm sorry, lady?'

'You were miles away, it appeared.'

The boy was embarrassed. 'I was just thinking what it would be like to go to Europe.'

He closed the book and the lady craned her neck around to see the title – *Treasures of the Major Cities of the Continent of Europe*.

'My, my, this is America, young man. Where everybody is supposed to want to go West.'

The boy's face remained in a serious set and his tone was cold when he replied: 'I'm not like everybody else, lady.'

She was a little taken aback. But then nodded. 'There's no harm in being different, I guess.' She took his place on the bench after he stood up. 'Good luck in whatever you want to do.'

'I appreciate it, lady. But I do not intend to rely on luck. I'll get to Europe by my own efforts.'

He tucked the book under his arm and touched the peak of his cap.

'I'm sure you will, young man. Bye bye.'

'Bye bye.'

She opened her purse and took out a paper sack filled with breadcrumbs. Birds flocked around her when she began to scatter the food.

The boy went from sight around a curve of the walk between the trees and the waterfront.

There would be many other days when he came here to read of and dream about what lay far to the East.

But events were to take him West.

CHAPTER ONE

FLOYD Channon heard the organ music break the perfect stillness which had previously filled the Arizona valley and for several seconds he expressed a scowl of fear. Then was embarrassed in his own company by his reaction to the totally unexpected sound. Next, as he recognised the melody, he spread a sardonic grin across his face.

The organist was playing the Death March.

With just the ghost of the grin still turning up the corners of his mouth and crinkling the skin at the sides of his eyes, he rose from the boulder upon which he had been seated for fifteen minutes or so. And went to where his jet black stallion was again cropping indifferently on a patch of dry scrub grass, after also being briefly alarmed by the abrupt intrusion of incongruous music into the long silence.

The handsome horse had lifted his head and pricked his ears to the sound, but otherwise had not moved. Remained, unfettered, on the spot where the man had commanded after dismounting to take a rest. Now, as the man slid a foot into the stirrup and swung smoothly up into the saddle, the stallion waited eagerly for a touch of heels to his flanks and a movement of the reins: sub-serviently anxious to respond instantly to the orders of the rider.

And Floyd Channon required an easy walking pace toward the source of the melancholy music. Which lay in the direction to which all the mid-morning shadows were pointed. North-west on a diagonal line across this broad valley which was cut through the Huachuca Moun-tains. A route which took the man away from his intended destination across the border in Mexico.

But the slow beat of the Death March, eerie in such a setting, had given Floyd Channon an idea. And although he looked forward to checking out whether or not his notion could be put into effect; he was easily able to con-tain his enthusiasm as he deftly steered his obedient mount across the dusty, boulder-strewn and cacti-featured slope towards the low ridge over which the organ music spilled. For patience was one of Floyd Channon's few virtues. Some said his only one. While others, who had stepped too far across the line which put them on the wrong side of this relentlessly tenacious man, had reason to regard his brand of patience as the very opposite to a virtue.

He was thirty years old and possessed the bearing which few men of his age could command: the smooth and easy self-assurance of a man who, if he did not have everything he wanted, knew where and how to get what-ever was lacking. He was as tall as a Texan is supposed to be – almost six and a half feet – and had a solid build that carried no fat surplus to the bodily need. His face was ruggedly handsome, clean shaven and stained an even shade of brown by the sun and winds of west Texas. The skin was free of blemishes, the eyes were a clear blue and his teeth were perfectly matched and exceptionally white.

Floyd Channon was dressed and his mount was equipped for the line of work they were in. Which was cowpunching, a long way from here on the Double-C range to the east of El Paso.

He wore a Texas-style high crown hat with a fabric Lone Star sewn on the side, a kerchief and shirt of cotton, denim pants and mule ear boots with work spurs: all of these a uniform grey. His batwing chaps were black, as was the gunbelt slung around his waist and hung on the right hip, with a holster into which was slotted a .44 Remington Frontier revolver. He rode on a Denver saddle double-cinched to the stallion, carrying a coiled lariat, a booted Winchester yellowboy rifle, two canteens, a pair of bags and with a bedroll lashed to the rear jockey. Although his clothing and equipment was workaday, it was all of the finest quality: much more expensive than the average cowpuncher could afford to buy.

But Floyd Channon was not an average cowpuncher.

As he neared the crest of the shallow slope, the mournful music was abruptly curtailed and apart from the slow clop of the stallion's hooves against the rock hard, dusty ground the valley became heavily silent again. Then, when he had reined the horse to a halt beside a towering four-pronged saguaro on the ridge, there was only the breathing of the man and the animal to be heard. Until a bell began to sound the death knell.

When Floyd Channon's eyes glinted and he exposed his gleaming white teeth in another grin of deep satisfaction.

The ground fell away sharply from where he sat astride the motionless horse, and at the foot of the steep, grotesquely eroded slope there was a shallow stream, which at this time of the year flowed sluggishly along a channel never wider than four feet. Fifty yards to the right of where he had halted the stallion, the stream curved away from the base of the high ground: arcing across a half mile strip of cultivated land to flow around the south side of a small community. A single street town at the end of a trail that ran arrow-straight northward along the valley bottom, bisecting scrub grass pastureland on which several small herds of mix-breed cattle were grazing.

The adobe and timber church, from the truncated tower of which the monotonous one-note clang of the death knell sounded, was at the southern end of the trail become street, built sideways across it to block it off. To the south of the church, spreading from its arch-windowed wall to the high water bank of the stream was the cemetery. Where, among headstones and crosses, a freshly dug grave waited to receive whoever was the subject of the funeral service in the church. A service attended by a great many of the town's citizens, Floyd Channon realised, as he dragged a shirt sleeve across his brow to wipe away beads of sweat. Maybe even everybody, for there was not a sign of life along the wide street to be seen from his elevated vantage point. A street without sidewalks, flanked by single storey buildings of adobe and timber and a mixture of the two. Stores and houses for the most part, constructed to serve their purpose and, seen from this distance, entirely lacking in fancy frills.

Again the black stallion responded instantly to the demands of the rider, to pick his way carefully down the treacherously steep slope. Then, at the bottom, the horse was allowed to drink some of the crystal-clear water from the stream: as the bell ceased to sound and the shuffling of many pairs of feet could be heard within the church. Muted by distance and then falling into a regular cadence

14

as a man's voice, deep and richly toned, began to recite the Thirty-Ninth Psalm.

The stallion was moving again, away from the stream along a direct line for the end of the street when the preacher came around the corner of the church, hands clasped and head bowed, speaking the words of the psalm from memory. Immediately behind him came four pallbearers with the casket carried on their shoulders. And, in back of them, the mourners.

Upwards of a hundred. Men, women and children. Moving slowly in a column four abreast. Too many to gather at the graveside, so that most held back at the edge of the cemetery. While just six men followed the preacher and the casket to align themselves across the newly-dug hole from the heap of displaced earth.

The approaching stranger was seen for the first time and there was a stir of interest among those mourners at the side of the cemetery. But almost immediately all attention reverted to the interment as the casket was lowered on ropes into the earth. And, the psalm finished, the preacher began to say in a louder voice: 'Man that is born of a woman hath but a short time to live, and is full of misery. He cometh up and is cut down like a . . .'

The pallbearers, their chore done, backed discreetly away. Everyone bowed their heads. Floyd Channon reined in his horse, took off his hat and held it against his chest.

A fly alighted on the tip of his nose and he rasped through clenched teeth: 'Get off me, you sonofabitch!' Jutted out his lower lip and expelled breath to send the fly buzzing angrily away. Then, patiently, he waited for the burial to run its course, filling in the time by surveying the youngest and firmest looking women among the mourners. Indifferently aware that, close to, probably

15

not one of them would merit more than a glance from him under normal circumstances.

Then, the religious aspect of the burial was over. One of the men at the graveside – the youngest and tallest – put on his hat and shook hands with the preacher. It was a narrow-brimmed, high crowned black hat. And he wore a long frock coat of the same sombre colour. A black shirt and necktie, too. Floyd Channon noticed as he urged the stallion to carry him closer to the cemetery: from which the main body of mourners was dispersing, while the preacher and the five other men at the side of the grave seemd to be engaged in a mild disagreement with the young mortician. But the outnumbered man won the point and the others started making their way between the old graves to leave the cemetery: paying only brief attention to the tall rider astride the stallion.

The young man dressed entirely in black gave no indication that he was aware of the approaching stranger, as he picked up a long-handled shovel from the ground and began to put the dirt back into the hole.

Floyd Channon halted his horse and dismounted on the bank of the stream. Stopped to stoop and moisten his hands which he rubbed over his sweat-greasy face, then approached the last man at the funeral on foot. There was one thud of earth against earth to every other foot-fall by the newcomer.

'Help you?' the man with the shovel asked, not interrupting his chore or looking up from it.

'I reckon you're the undertaker hereabouts?'

Another shovelful of dirt thudded into the grave. 'My father was.'

'I'm real sorry.'

'I appreciate the sentiment.'

'You've taken over from him, it seems to me.'

'It's what he wanted. But what he wanted isn't impor-

16

tant anymore. Least I could do was bury him, though.'

'I'm real anxious to have a casket made.'

'Last one I ever intend to make is under this dirt. There are a few plain pine coffins back at the funeral parlour. Give you a bargain price. Part of my closing down sale.'

Floyd Channon grunted his disinterest in this. 'I ain't looking for a bargain, feller. Want something made of the finest materials. Mahogany, maybe. Silver handles and hinges. Silk or satin trimmings inside. Lead-lined if you can do it.'

The young undertaker interrupted his chore with the grave only half filled in. And surveyed the big Texan curiously: even doubtfully, as if suspecting the seriousness of the man's request.

'You're talking real big money.'

A nod. 'And you're talking to Floyd Channon. That's one of the Channons off the Double-C range, way the other side of El Paso from here.'

The undertaker was in his mid-twenties. A lanky six footer with a thin, angular face. Blond haired and green eyed. With good looks close to the far end of the range from the ruggedness of the Texan's features.

Channon realised his family name meant nothing to the man, but sensed he was interested in the proposition. Even though the black-clad mortician said: 'I'm planning to leave for Europe soon as the business is sold.'

The Texan nodded. 'You reckon you could make the kind of casket I need – and have plenty left over for your trip – out of a fee of a thousand dollars?'

The undertaker's interest deepened. 'I'd be over-charging you, Mr Channon.'

A shake of the head as the stranger from Texas reached into a hip pocket and withdrew a roll of bills. 'You didn't set the charge. I named my price. Half now and half when you've made what I need.'

'It'll take time.'

Now Channon nodded, as he peeled off some bills from the roll. Four centuries and two fifties. He held them out across the grave and after a moment's hesitation they were taken.

'Take the time, feller.' He turned to return across the cemetery to where the stallion obediently waited.

'Hey, Mr Channon! Where do I pick up the deceased?'

The Texan paused to glance back at the perplexed young undertaker. 'You don't have to concern yourself with that, feller. I'll haul in the carcase.' He patted the butt of the Remington jutting from his holster. And sent a globule of saliva at the arid ground. 'Just as soon as I've slaughtered it.'

CHAPTER TWO

FLOYD Channon was conscious of being watched as, astride the stallion again, he backtracked over the flat land and then dismounted to lead the animal up the steep incline. He cast an eye across at the town twice. The first time saw that the undertaker was working at filling in the grave again, while a group of men approached him and frequently glanced over towards the departing stranger. The second time the lanky, blond-haired, black-clad young man was still at work with the shovel and his fellow citizens were withdrawing from the cemetery. There was something ill-tempered in the way they moved, spoke to each other and spared the occasional glance for the undertaker and the stranger.

And the Texan grinned. There had not been time for the man with the shovel to explain the reason for the stranger's brief visit to town. Maybe just enough time to tell his inquisitive neighbours to mind their own business.

Then Channon was at the ridge beside the saguaro again and he remounted the stallion. Rode him down the more gentle slope to where he had rested on the rock, unaware that there was a town in the vicinity. On beyond this, covering ground that was new to him as he headed slowly but relentlessly south through the Huachuca Mountains valley.

At midday he rested himself and his horse. Ate some jerked beef stew washed down with tepid water from a canteen. At nightfall he made camp and lit a fire to cook a hot meal and brew coffee. He had seen no international boundary marker, but guessed he was now in Mexico. Maybe two days' ride from where he was headed, if the information he had been given in El Paso was good. If it wasn't, his patience would stand him in good stead. The undertaker would just have to wait a while longer for the second payment.

He damped the fire without putting it out and then bedded down. Slept soundly and awoke at first light. Had just coffee for breakfast while he shaved, and was in the saddle and out of sight of the place where he had camped before the sun pushed its leading arc above the eastern ridges of the Sierra Madre.

It had been a long ride from the Double-C range but Floyd Channon had ridden longer trails than this. Tougher ones, too. Riding and working as hard as any of the hired hands up the Goodnight-Loving Trail to Cheyenne. Eating the dust of vast herds of longhorns. Busting herd quitters, turning stampedes, running off rustlers and making sure no hungry Indians ever filled their bellies with Double-C beef.

So this trip was an easy one. Little more arduous to a man like Floyd Channon than the Sunday afternoon buggy rides he used to take: with Emily Jane on the shaded seat beside him and a picnic basket in the boot.

The information from the Mexican at the stinking cantina in El Paso had been good. And when he realised this, Floyd Channon grinned for the first time since riding

20

away from the one street town north of the border. Then he made camp, even though it was still only mid-afternoon. He did not light a fire. Nor did he give tacit expression to his satisfaction after the initial response to finding the place he had been looking for.

The area where he unsaddled the horse and made a few preparations for a patient wait was some thirty feet back from the mouth of the gully. A narrow, twisting gully with fifty foot high sides which he had followed for perhaps half a mile: the ground constantly rising beneath the slow moving hooves of the stallion. When he saw he was approaching its end, he reined in his mount, swung out of the saddle and slid the yellowboy Winchester from the boot. Then moved cautiously forward to check on the terrain that lay beneath the cloudless sky which was all he could see between the twin faces of grey rock at the gully's mouth.

From the moment he had known he must be across the border in Mexico, he had shown this brand of caution, since the landscape of the mountain country was such that he might ride openly into the place where he wanted his presence to remain a secret – until he was ready to make it known.

On those previous occasions when his wariness had proved to be unnecessary, the blue eyes that surveyed a fresh expanse of empty terrain had never shown anything but resignation. Which was all they expressed now as, after taking care of his horse, he went to the mouth of the gully again. This time carrying his bedroll instead of the rifle, which he set down at the base of the shaded rockface, and sat on it. Then, with his chin resting on his fists which were wedged against his folded up-knees, he gazed bleakly at the man he intended to kill.

The man, whose name was Arturo Loera, was a long way off. At least two miles out on the high country plain that spread to the south of the gully mouth. Just a miniature silhouette moving wearily against the grey dusty surface of the vast plain. He was weary because it was blisteringly hot out there. And had been even hotter earlier in the day which in something less than two hours would reach its evening. A day, like many others, during which Arturo Loera had worked hard on the building project he had set himself. And continued to work at it for as long as the daylight held and Floyd Channon could see him.

The Mexican was building a house – a small scale hacienda that he dreamed of expanding in the passing of time. Maybe even to the extent that it would become as large and prosperous as the Double-C range of the Channons.

And he had made a fine start, the watching Texan allowed, as he maintained his stoic surveillance of the lone man throughout what was left of the afternoon. And recalled what he had been told by the fat bartender in the evil smelling cantina back in El Paso. Six months ago.

'Arturo Loera, *Señor* Channon? *Si,* he was a customer of mine. But if all the customers were like this one, I would not have a business here. He come once a week. Maybe not so often sometimes. A single tequila, it lasts him the whole time he is here. Not like other Mexicans who work on the Double-C. Your father, he pays well for his hands. And all who use my place, they spend well. On the liquor, the food, the women. But not Arturo Loera.

'But I do not mind this, *señor*. Once I was as young as he. I had hopes and dreams. But I wasted the time and the money. So that today, I have only this hole in the wall. But that Arturo Loera, he will do better. I have spoken with him many times. After those other Mexicans he work with on the Double-C had grown bored with what he talks of.

'Some land, *señor*. In the Sierra Madre below the border with Territory of Arizona. A land without an owner for it appears to have no value. But Arturo Loera, he says there is water beneath the land. Which can be pumped to the surface so that grass can be made to grow. Enough grass to feed many cattle.

'If he has gone, *Señor* Channon, this is where you will find him. With enough money to begin building his dream. Enough to begin working for himself on his own land. In the way that your father did, long ago. When the Double-C was little more than a shack beside a water-hole, no?'

Floyd Channon had made no reply.

The fat bartender added: 'This young man, he has much admiration for your father, *señor*.'

'Something else, too.'

The atmosphere in the dimly-lit cantina had suddenly got as ugly as the stink of the place. When, by his expression and tone of voice, Floyd Channon revealed more than a hint of just why he was asking after the Mexican hand who had left the Double-C spread without notice.

'Something is wrong, *señor*?' The bartender licked his fleshy lips nervously and shifted his small eyes quickly back and forth across the sockets. But it was three o'clock in the morning and every other customer had left. Even the two whores were in their tiny back rooms, sleeping off the effects of too much liquor and the exhaustion of faked passion. He had heard second and third-hand tales of how harshly this Floyd Channon dealt with men who crossed him. But until now, during this first meeting with a member of the Channon family, the Mexican had dis-counted the stories. Vindictive rumours spread by lazy

23

drunks without ambition who were jealous of the Channons.

This was the closest to a gentleman the Mexican had ever had in his cantina: until that moment when, by a change of tone and a slight alteration of facial expression, he seemed abruptly to become the epitome of evil.

'Nothing that concerns you, feller. Did he ever get more specific than somewhere in the Sierra Madre below the Arizona border?'

Floyd Channon had known what kind of anguish was gripping the mind of the fat bartender. For several minutes the Mexican had spoken in glowing, almost paternalistic, terms of a youngster he obviously had a deep feeling for. And only when it was too late did he realise the Texan's questions had an ulterior motive at their foundations.

'*Señor* Channon, I . . .'

The American leaned across the bar counter so that his face was only six inches from that of the Mexican. 'If I even think you're lying to me, feller, I'll cut out your tongue and ram it up your ass. *Comprender?*'

The bartender swallowed hard, nodded, and stammered out directions to the piece of land Arturo Loera planned to build on.

'Much obliged,' Floyd Channon said, straightening up and assuming the attitude which had earlier won the Mexican's confidence. And spoke in the same easy-going manner as he explained: 'Some chores around the Double-C are going to hold me to the spread for a few weeks, feller. So there'll be plenty of time to warn Loera that his dream's going to turn out to be a nightmare. If that happens, though, this entire world won't be big enough for the both of us.'

'He was just a customer, *Señor* Channon.' The flabby shoulders moved in a shrug. 'And not a good one, either.'

Shame sounded in the voice of the fat man. Then defiance when he added: 'But I will pray for him!'

In the doorway of the cantina, the Texan nodded. 'That's all right, feller. Even we Channons have always admitted that divine intervention is something we can't get the better of.'

It was as dark as it had been on that night in El Paso when Floyd Channon rose from the base of the gully side, carried his bedroll back to where the stallion was waiting, and saddled the horse. Not pitch black out on the high plain the sliver of a new moon shed silvery light from low in the western sky. To cast long shadows from the partially built hacienda: and from the horse and rider when they emerged from the gully mouth and headed toward the results of Arturo Loera's labours.

The house itself was long and low, with a flat roof which extended out from the front to provide daytime shade for the stoop. If the young Mexican were allowed to live and work the place, it was apparent he had plans to extend the main building with wings running out from either side – perhaps eventually to add a further section so that the whole place would enclose a courtyard. But he had gone as far as he needed with the living accommodation for the time being. And the work the Texan had watched him do today was on a stable block in back of the house. Using both adobe and timber from a nearby stack of materials. Adjacent to a pump tower with wind sails at the top.

There had not been the slightest breeze to turn the sails while the secret watcher looked on. But smoke had risen constantly from a stack at the side of a small shack at the base of the tower, obviously from the fire box of a steam pump. Drawing water from deep beneath the barren plain to stock a large, rectangular pool behind the half-finished stable block

Floyd Channon paid scant attention to the features of the hacienda-in-the-making as he came closer to the buildings. For, apart from his brief stopover at the small Arizona town, he had not allowed any side issues to cloud the main one which was the singleminded purpose of his long, lone ride from the established ranch east of El Paso to this embryonic spread in Mexico.

Thus did he concentrate his unblinking gaze upon one section of the façade of the house: a net curtained window that was squared by yellow lamplight and the closed door to the right of it. And as he rode, although he made no unnecessary noise, he did not attempt to mask the inevitable sounds of the stallion's slow approach.

He was two hundred feet from the front of the house, riding between lengths of cord pegged to the ground to mark out the positions of the future wings, when the clop of hooves was heard by the Mexican and Arturo Loera's head and torso were silhouetted at the lamplit window.

Floyd Channon acknowledged that he had seen the man by raising a hand to flick all four fingers at the underside of the brim. A brim that was wide enough to cast a deep shadow over his face – which wore an expression at odds with the easy gesture of friendly greeting.

The Mexican moved away from the window.

The American dropped his hand to fist it around the frame of the booted Winchester. Then slid the rifle out of the leather, thumbing back the hammer behind a breech that was already slotted with an unfired shell. And continued to close with the front of the house, the barrel of the Winchester resting across the back of the horn.

Fifty feet short of the gap in the stoop railing, he reined the stallion to a halt.

The door across from the gap swung open with just the rattle of the catch – no bolts had been shot. A widening wedge of light angled out over the stoop. The tall, slim frame of Arturo Loera became totally exposed: less distinctly silhouetted against the dimmer light which spilled from the room to the right of the hallway in which he stood.

'*De nada, amigo,*' the Mexican greeted warmly.

And made to step off the threshold and on to the stoop.

Floyd Channon swung the Winchester and squeezed the trigger.

Arturo Loera was hit in the belly in mid-stride. He set his leading foot down on the stoop and made a rasping sound through his teeth, which were still exposed in what was no longer a smile of friendly greeting. Then he splayed both hands to the blood-spilling wound in his belly and looked down at the dark stain that was blossoming over his white shirt and pants.

Floyd Channon pumped the lever action of the repeater – the only movement made by the man seated astride the motionless horse.

Arturo Loera snapped up his head at the metallic sounds and for a split second still expressed total non-comprehension. But then he recognised his night caller.

The rifle cracked out a second time. A heart shot that sent the Mexican backwards across the threshold. Killed him on his feet so that he was spared the much milder shock of his rear, shoulders and the back of his head slamming to the floor.

'Twice you got it wrong about me, you sonofabitch,' Floyd Channon drawled, as he worked the action to send another empty shell-case spinning to the ground. 'I ain't welcome here at all.'

CHAPTER THREE

WITHIN ten minutes of the cold-blooded killing of Arturo Loera, there was little sign outside the hacienda that an act of violence had taken place. Some freshly made imprints of hooves and booted feet in the dust and a few spots of dried blood on the stoop boarding. But to see these and read anything into them, a person coming to the place would first have had to be suspicious: next, skilled in the art of deciphering something from virtually nothing.

Inside the house, there was a little more blood than out: splashed across the floor of the hallway by the impact of the twice gunshot body when it fell. But with the door to the parlour closed, just a crack of light showed below it and failed to reach the bloodied area.

A diminished level of light, for the wick of a kerosene lamp which stood on the mantelshelf above the stone fireplace was now turned low. So low that the corners of the big room were in darkness. Seated on a rod-back chair in one of these dark corners was Floyd Channon, with the Winchester resting across his thighs. Closer to the lamp, to the left of the empty fireplace, Arturo Loera was slumped in a Boston rocker: the bullet holes in his body concealed by a blanket which draped him from shoulders to knees. The blanket was kept in place by the weight of his chin resting on his chest. He appeared to be asleep and only the absence of any sound of breathing betrayed that it was an eternal rest that now encompassed him.

Upon entering the room, the Texan had taken note only of those aspects of its contents which could be of use to him. Just as, out in the shell of the stable block, he had paid attention only to those signs which showed him two horses were normally enstalled there. And a wagon was often moved to and from a parking place beside the block.

He fed and watered the stallion, then unsaddled him before entering the house and fixing up the dead man in the rocker, lowering the wick of the lamp and shifting the rod-back chair into the darkened corner. This in a room that was in keeping with the unfinished state of the hacienda as a whole. Adequately furnished for the basic requirements of a room to live in, but as yet lacking the personal touches that turned a house into a home.

The bedroom from which he had brought the blanket was in much the same condition.

He did not intrude further into the house for as yet there was no need. He hoped such a need would not arise, but if it did whatever provisions were in the kitchen larder would run out before his patience. And he had been hungry before. If the stench of the Mexican's decomposing flesh became too overpowering to take . . . ?

But this was a line of conjecture that he elected to abandon as futile. Choosing to believe that the two place settings at the pine dining-table in another darkened corner of the room were not permanent fixtures – that the eating utensils had been put there because the Mexican fully expected to have company for supper.

Floyd Channon lost track of time as he sat and waited. His mind a blank because he had no wish to recall the worst of the past: and no desire to anticipate a patiently awaited pleasure of the near future.

So, when he heard the far-off sounds of a wagon hauled by a two-horse team, he knew only that it was still night and that the low flame of the lamp had not yet exhausted all the oil in the reservoir.

He rose from the chair, flexed his muscles after the period of inactivity and sat down again. Thumbed back the hammer of the Winchester and curled his index finger to the trigger.

The wagon was coming from the south-east, the team hauling it at a walking pace.

He pursed his lips and inhaled and exhaled air with a low whistle as the sounds of the approaching wagon swelled in volume. Began to breathe silently again after it was halted out back of the place. He expected to hear a call for the Mexican to go help with the horses, but none came. Instead, just the sounds of footfalls, across the rear yard, round the side and then along the front of the house. A quick, excited tread.

Floyd Channon tilted the Winchester toward the ceiling, resting the stockplate on a thigh and holding it with one hand curled around the frame.

Footfalls rang out more clearly on the stoop boarding. The front door opened with the rattle of the catch.

The Winchester was now taken in a two-handed grip, levelled from the shoulder with the right side of the Texan's face pressed to the smooth wood of the stock. The man's teeth gleamed faintly in the extreme periphery of the lamplight's glow: bared as part of a grimace of anguish.

The door from the hallway opened.

'Wake up, sleepy head. Say hello to your . . .'

'Hello, Emily Jane.'

Her voice, filled with love, happiness and excitement, had faltered a moment before he announced his presence – as she sensed that the familiar room contained an unseen evil.

'Arturo!' she shrieked, held rigid on the threshold of the room: wanting desperately to lunge toward the body trapped in the chair by death, but rooted to the spot by the certain knowledge of the Mexican's inability to be protected or offer protection from the threat in the darkened corner.

'Goodbye, Emily Jane.'

Just a single shot. Sounding, in the confines of the spartanly furnished room, louder than the two fired outside. Blasting a bullet through the lower slope of her left breast and into her heart. Sending her staggering backwards across the hallway. To bounce as a corpse off the far wall and fall spreadeagled on her belly to the floor.

Floyd Channon rose from the chair and pumped the action of the Winchester to eject the spent shell and jack a live one into the breech. Then stood for long moments, his eyes closed while his lips remained parted. Until every muscle in his big frame started to ache from the strain of holding so still – and the threat of tears receded.

Then he made his preparations to leave. He took the blanket off the corpse of Arturo Loera with a jerk that set the rocker rocking and caused the dead Mexican to slump limply to the side over an arm. And went into the hallway to cover the woman: this act performed as irreverently as the first. Just a trace of the earlier anguish touched his features as he kept his head averted – so as not to look at the beautiful face, long blonde hair and work-clothed slimness of the woman's body.

He went outside to the stable to saddle his stallion. Then took both geldings from the traces of the flatbed wagon laden with furniture and watered them. Saddled the grey and led this with his stallion to the front of the house. He cut lengths from his lariat to tie the blanket around the woman's corpse, draped it over the saddle of the grey and secured it tightly in place.

Then he sat down on the edge of the stoop and ate a meal of jerked beef and cold beans from the can. Drank some water from one of his canteens and for the first time became aware of the chill which night had brought to the mountains. So, before linking the two horses together with a rope lead-line, he took a knee-length, fur-lined overcoat from his bedroll and put it on, turning up the collar so that it brushed the underside of his hat brim at the back and sides.

Only then did he mount the stallion and begin the long ride back toward the border and the one-street town on the other side.

Not once, after the putrefaction process began to become malodorously apparent during the hottest part of the following day, did Floyd Channon consider burying the rotting corpse out there in the wilderness. It had been a spur of the moment decision to arrange for a decent funeral, born out of the accident of his being within earshot of another interment.

But he was glad he had had the notion. He owed Emily Jane that much.

CHAPTER FOUR

IT was a little after midday when Floyd Channon came within sight of the small Arizona town which looked as deserted as when he had first seen it. Another similar feature was an open grave in the cemetery out back of the church. But today there was no sound of an organ playing the Death March or of the bell tolling the death knell. Nor would there be.

The people were eating or getting ready to eat, and as he rode closer he could smell the appetising aroma of hot food mingling with the fumes of woodsmoke that rose through the still air like dark columns from almost every chimney. But even when he was on the street, having ridden between a corner of the church and a small house, these everyday smells of a peaceful community were not strong enough to keep the stink of the woman's decomposing flesh from his nostrils.

There were four houses to either side of this southern end of the street, each of them with a garden enclosed by picket fences. Beyond, on the eastern side, was a hardware store, a grocery, a bakery, a meat market,

3

barbers, bank, three more houses, a saloon, drugstore and a blacksmiths. Facing these across the sixty foot wide, rutted and dusty street was a meeting hall, a candy store, drapers, funeral parlour, laundry, six houses and a school.

Many of the business premises incorporated the name Fairfax in their signs. The sign above the door and black-draped window of the funeral parlour read: Barnaby Gold and Son.

By the time the Texan had reached the front of this establishment, a large proportion of the citizens of Fairfax were uneasily aware of his return to town. And peered surreptitiously from curtained windows and half-open doorways, wrinkling their noses as the stench of long-dead flesh assaulted their nostrils.

Floyd Channon, aware of being the centre of attention but totally ignoring it, swung out of his saddle and untied the lead-line. Whispered words from the buildings along both sides of the street disturbed the peace like the buzzing of a swarm of flies.

A child's voice demanded: 'What's happenin', Ma?'

'Hold your tongue and eat, boy!' a woman snapped.

'But . . .'

A hand cracked against flesh and there was a cry of pain.

'Do like your Ma tells you!' a man growled.

The lanky, youthful, blond-haired inheritor of the funeral parlour opened the door. Today he was dressed in old denim pants and a cotton shirt, sweat and dirt stained.

'Reckon you didn't tell folks about me planning on coming back, Gold?'

'Just did as you asked, Mr Channon. It's out back in the workshop. You want to see it?'

34

The Texan took the roll from his hip pocket and peeled off some bills. Ten fifties this time.

The youngster emerged from the doorway and took the money with one hand and the lead-line with the other: as the taller, broader man shook his head.

'A Channon is as good as his word and expects those he does business with to be likewise. If he gets cheated, he knows. And the cheater gets to pay.' He thrust out his bottom lip and blew air up over his sweat-greasy face. 'Need to slake my thirst. See you got the grave dug. You'll send word over to the saloon when everythin's ready for the burying?'

'Take a little while to prepare the deceased, Mr Channon. The longer the time since death, the more work is necessary to give the corpse a . . .'

The Texan took hold of the reins of the stallion and gave a negligent wave with his free hand. 'That's your business, feller. You want to pretty her up, you do it. I ain't gonna look at her again.'

For the first time since he opened the door to see and smell what was draped over the saddle of the grey gelding, the young Gold expressed surprise.

'The deceased is a lady?'

'Used to think so,' Channon answered, and spat into a wheel rut on the street. 'Turned out she was nothing but a whore. So I don't figure on any preaching and organ music and bell ringing. I'll wait to hear from you.'

He turned away and led the stallion diagonally across the street to hitch him to the rail out front of the Fairfax Saloon. While the young undertaker led the corpse-burdened gelding into the alley between the funeral parlour and the laundry.

The shocked citizenry of the town, most of whom had been able to overhear the conversation between the two men, withdrew from their vantage points.

Floyd Channon pushed through the batwing doors of the small saloon after the bartender and his only other customer had got back to where they had been before the Texan's return to Fairfax caused such a stir.

'Beer, a bottle of rye and a shot glass.'

He dropped into a chair at the table nearest to the doorway.

It was one of only five tables in the place, which was about twenty by twenty-five feet in area with the bar counter running across the rear wall. There was sawdust on the floor, cobwebs hanging from the ceiling rafters and a thousand and one stains on the adobe walls. The air smelled of tobacco smoke, liquor and sweat. All stale.

The bartender who delivered the requested beer and whiskey to the table was a heavily built man of sixty with an untidy black beard, a bald head and a belly that overhung the top of the leather apron he wore. He also wore a collarless, sleeveless shirt that tightly contoured his almost feminine chest.

'Buck and a half, Mr Channon,' he growled and was given a five.

'Keep the change.'

'Didn't I tell you that family was known for bein' free with the money, Jeb?'

This from the man who stood at the bar with a half-empty glass of flat beer. A scrawny old timer who was more than eighty. Wearing what looked like hand-me-down pants and shirt that were three sizes too large for him. He had grey hair and a beard that was neatly trimmed.

'Much obliged,' Jeb responded as he pocketed the five dollars. 'Ain't sayin' I disbelieved what Jack Cater told me, Mr Channon. But rumours, much as haircuts and shaves, are a barber man's stock-in-trade. Wouldn't you say?'

36

There was a spittoon beside each table and after he had taken a mouthful of beer the Texan scored a perfect hit with a stream of dust-flecked saliva. Then: 'Don't plan on saying much of anything until I've slacked my thirst, feller.'

'Yessir,' Jack Cater went on when the bartender was back behind his counter. 'I've barbered in a lot of cow-towns from the south west up through Kansas and even the Dakotas. And any hand who ever worked the Double-C over to Texas, he spoke high of it. Had to work their butts off, but any puncher worth his salt is ready to do that. Iffen the pay's good. And the Channons, they pay top rate. Hire the best cooks, provide the best grub and got bunkhouses and line shacks on the spread that are a damn sight better than some places call themselves hotels.'

Floyd Channon finished the beer and started on the whiskey, trying to keep his mind as blank as his expression while he listened to what the town barber was saying: his back to both men. But after the third shot of hard liquor, he began to smile pensively and this was a reflection of the pleasant thoughts which seeped into his mind. This as Jack Cater got into his stride, recalling from the distant and more recent past specific instances of how the Channons and the Double-C had won and maintained respect among cattlemen from the humblest hand up to fellow barons.

The steadily-drinking Texan had heard some of the stories and they were told accurately. So it figured the ones he was hearing for the first time were also on the level. He recognised the names of some men and places, and had even been directly involved with some of the incidents.

Then the barber seemed to be through with his remi-niscences of the Channon family and its fair treatment of Double-C employees and in the ensuing silence a clock struck to mark the hour of two. The pleasant double chime from a room in the back of the saloon jerked the Texan's mind out of the past. He saw there was just an inch of liquor remaining in the bottom of the bottle. And became aware of sound and movement out on the street – signs that Fairfax was going about its afternoon business. But there were still just the two customers in the saloon.

'Course,' Jack Cater went on, his tone lower than before, 'by the same token, the Channons is also known for not takin' too kind to folks that cross them.'

'Ain't it time you got back to your parlour, Jack?' Jeb said quickly. Uneasily.

The last traces of the smile drained out of the Texan's face as he poured the final shot from the bottle to the glass, stood up and turned.

'All right, feller,' he said, his voice a little slurred. He was conscious of this, so took great care not to stumble as he made his way between the tables and chairs to the bar. 'I'm not about to take offence at what's the honest truth.'

He leaned his elbows on the bartop and hooked a heel over the rail, ten feet down the counter from where Jack Cater and Jeb stood. He set the glass in front of him and peered into a past that seemed to be overlaid on the bottle-lined shelves fixed to the wall.

'I've known a few small towns in my time. And how they can be real dull unless people bring in some news from outside.'

'You got no need to tell us your business, Mr Channon,' Jeb said.

'I feel the friggin' need, feller!' the Texan snarled.

The barber glowered at the bartender. Said to the man down the counter: 'I listen good as I can talk.'

Floyd Channon nodded his satisfaction with this. 'The woman was in real bad trouble. Run up a month's rent in a hotel at El Paso and didn't have the money to pay it. The feller that had the hotel, he was fixing to get her to work it off in his bed. Another feller wanted to pick up her tab and put her into a Mex bordello. But she got lucky. I heard the shindig, laid out the two fellers arguing over her, paid the tab and took her back to the ranch.'

'Real pretty, was she, Mr Channon?' the barber said into a pause.

'Beautiful, more like,' the Texan answered. 'Just twenty years old and the most beautiful thing I ever saw.' There was another short silence, which he ended himself with a sigh. 'She said she could cook and it turned out she could. Real well. And that's what she did at the house, for the family. To pay back what I ante-ed up for her at the hotel.

'The old man, my two brothers and even my sister, they took to her. And they were real pleased when she and me reached an understanding. Helped me when I started to build a place for us down in the south-east section of the Double-C range. Had the place more finished than the Mex . . . '

His voice trailed off and he shook his head to rid his mind of the memory of Arturo Loera's hacienda. While the bartender and the barber exchanged quizzical glances.

'Anyway, needed to go up to San Antone with the old man. Land deal business. When I got back, she'd gone. Along with ten thousand dollars cash from the old man's safe. And a Mex cowhand no one even knew she'd ever seen.'

'Hot damn,' Jack Cater rasped.

'Ten friggin' grand,' Jeb added and whistled.

Floyd Channon raised his glass, drank half its contents and set it down again. 'Had to be taken care of. But round-up needed to be done first. Both out of the way now. Twenty thousand head of prime beef are being herded up to Denver. And two more people got paid out for crossing a Channon.'

'Two?' Jeb posed. 'You only brought in the one body that I saw.'

The Texan finished the whiskey. 'The Mex had a dream, feller. Left him dead where he was building it. Guess you could say the woman gave me . . .'

Again he allowed a sentence to hang half-finished in the hot, stale-smelling air of the small saloon.

'Young Barnaby Gold looks about ready to start the buryin', Mr Channon,' Jack Cater said, nodding across the saloon toward the dusty window.

'Much obliged.'

He pushed away from the counter and turned around. Moved toward the batwings feeling a lot less drunk: but mentally and physically drained from reliving the pleasures, pains and humiliations of the recent past.

'Best of luck to you,' Jeb offered.

The barber added: 'Give my best to any of the Double-C hands that might recall I give them a shave or a haircut.'

The Texan went out through the batwings, stepping from the shaded heat of the building into the glaring brand that beat down on the street.

'Plan on forgetting I was ever in this place,' he murmured as he blinked against the bright sunlight.

CHAPTER FIVE

THE street was virtually deserted once more. Except for
Floyd Channon and his stallion and Barnaby Gold Junior
and his hearse and two-horse team.

It was an impressive looking vehicle for such a small
town mortician to own. A circular hearse with glass panels
in the sides and pieces of curved glass at the front and
rear. The woodwork painted in shiny black with silver
trimmings at each corner. Clipped feather plumes along
the top of each side. The seat upon which the undertaker
sat, detached from the curved glass front panel of the
body, was draped with black and silver hammer cloth.

The two horses which drew it were also jet black and
had plumes in their bridles.

Barnaby Gold had changed into the sombre garb of
his trade.

The casket which rested between silver rails in the
hearse met, from its outside appearance, the specifications
that Floyd Channon had ordered.

'You're doing her proud,' he said as he led the stallion

41

across the street to where the hearse was halted at the front of the funeral parlour.

'It's what you asked for, Mr Channon,' Gold told him impassively.

'Didn't figure you'd have a special rig for . . . '

'It's the only one. Shall we get started for the cemetery?'

The Texan squinted up at the black-garbed younger man, whose attitude was suddenly so cold. Decided Emily Jane's body had not decomposed to the extent where Gold had failed to be moved by such a waste of beautiful young womanhood. He nodded.

'Yeah, let's get it over with, feller. So I can get back to Texas.'

'And I can start for Europe,' Gold countered, flicking the reins to set the team moving.

Floyd Channon took off his hat and walked behind the slow-rolling hearse, leading his stallion.

With a single exception, those who now watched the cortege move along the brightly sunlit street did so with greater surreptitiousness than when they had followed the Texan's entrance into town.

The lone man who did not hide far back from windows and doorways was the elderly, slightly-built preacher. Who stood in the arched entrance of his church, hands clasped to his chest and head bowed.

'I said she didn't deserve any praying over, feller,' Channon growled.

'The Reverend Baxter sees some good in everyone,' Gold answered. 'I didn't fix for him to be around.'

He steered the team to the left, to pass between the church and the fence of the last house on the east side of the cemetery where four sombrely dressed men were waiting.

'And these fellers?' the Texan asked as he quickened

his pace to move up alongside the slowing hearse: aware of the animosity which had been briefly glared at him before the quartet of men went around the other side of the hearse to get to the rear of it.

'You asked for a lead-lined casket, Mr Channon,' Gold answered as he applied the brake lever and hitched the reins around it. Climbed down on the side where the irritable Texan stood. 'I asked for some help to carry it. It was the men's own idea to dress in mourning.'

'All right to unload it, Mr Gold?' one of the pall-bearers asked gruffly.

'Sure.'

The rear glass panel was a door which hinged open to the right. As it was opened and the heavy casket was slid out along a track with grunts and rasped sounds of exertion, Floyd Channon massaged his forehead. And seemed to be on the point of spitting until he realised he and the youthful undertaker were walking side-by-side between graves.

'Shit,' he growled and the expletive caused him no self-consciousness. 'Had a snort more than I should have over at the saloon, feller. Not thinking straight. You've done a real fine job.'

Since the Texan had seen Emily Jane's grave earlier, two stout lengths of timber had been placed across the hole, with ropes running along their tops.

'Appreciate you appreciate the service, Mr Channon,' Barnaby Gold replied levelly as he stooped to readjust the distance between the timbers and ropes.

Then he stood back and beckoned for the Texan to also clear a path for the four pallbearers, whose sweat-beaded faces were contorted with grimaces of strain as they struggled to remain at their full heights under the great weight on their shoulders. The burden was lowered on to the timbers by the solid silver handles that glinted brightly in the sunlight against the deep sheen of the polished mahogany.

'It's usual to remove the hat,' Gold said.

The pallbearers had been hatless since sliding the casket from the hearse. And now the undertaker was bareheaded, after going down on his haunches to withdraw the timbers from beneath the casket, the four nameless men taking its weight again with the ropes.

Standing directly across the grave from Gold, Floyd Channon showed a contrite expression as he hurriedly took off his hat and held it to his chest.

He muttered in self anger: 'Addled brain!'

'Fine,' Gold said in instruction and the casket was lowered carefully into the grave.

When it came to rest in the depths of the arid earth, the ropes were hauled clear.

'Ashes to ashes,' a pallbearer said mournfully.

'Dust to dust,' said another.

'May God have mercy on your soul.'

'Rest in peace.'

The Texan had closed his eyes and bowed his head. Only opened them at the sound of a small quantity of soil hitting the lid of the casket. And saw, through a blur of not quite held back tears, that Barnaby Gold had tossed a first handful of earth into the grave. This as the pallbearers backed away, their chore completed.

He reached for the hip pocket bulged out by the roll of bills: as he replaced his hat and brushed a shirt sleeve across his moist eyes.

'I'll pay for the extra expense I hadn't figured on.'

Gold shook his head as he put on his high crowned black hat and stooped to pick up the long-handled shovel from behind the heap of displaced earth.

'The men were retained by the business to do what they did, Mr Channon. There's no additional charge.'

44

And now he began to sweat as he set about filling-in the grave, his black clothing becoming layered with grey dust motes that billowed up with each shovelful of soil sent into the hole.

The Texan watched him in silence for long seconds, until the pallbearers had gone from sight beyond the church: and the steadily working undertaker was the sole source of hostility in the marker-featured cemetery.

Then: 'I loved her, Gold. Maybe if I hadn't loved her so much, I wouldn't have needed to kill her.'

He started out speaking with an angry tone. Finished melancholic.

'Thought you came close to crying, Mr Channon,' the undertaker answered without interrupting the rhythm of his chore.

'You saw her. And I guess you could still see how beautiful she was?'

'I fixed it so she was smiling. I can't disagree with you. Loveliest woman I've ever seen.'

Floyd Channon peered down into the rapidly filling grave in which there was no longer any sight of the elaborate casket.

'But she used what she had to lie and cheat. If it had just been me . . . ' He shrugged. 'But she tricked the whole Channon family. I brought her to the Double-C and so it was my responsibility. She hoodwinked the whole bunch of us. Took the old man for ten grand and run off with a Mex cowhand.'

He was dull-eyed and dull-voiced: staring down into the dust-exploding grave and, as in the saloon, seeing images of the past pictured there.

'The old man didn't have to tell me. But he did. The Channons couldn't let a thing like that pass, Gold. Nobody has ever crossed us and got away with it. So I had to go after her and the Mex. What I did when I

45

found them was up to me. Like I say . . . if I hadn't loved her . . . maybe I'd have done it differently.'

He sighed, as the last of the earth was put back in the form of an elongated mound.

'Gelded the Mex that stole her. Took what was left of the money. Maybe beat up on her some.'

'Channon business isn't mine,' Barnaby Gold said, hoisting the shovel to his shoulder and starting back for the hearse. 'There's no need for me to know . . . '

'Channons aren't cold-hearted killers, feller!' the Texan cut in harshly as he moved alongside the shorter, slighter, younger man. 'We've got a fine reputation in cattle raising circles and outside. It's important to us it doesn't get muddied up by half-truths and ill-informed rumours. Sure I killed a woman and I don't give a damn who knows it. But it's real important to me that people who know it know just why I did it.'

They had reached the side of the hearse.

'If anyone asks me, Mr Channon, I'll tell them.'

Gold brought the shovel down from his shoulder and began to twist it in both hands: unscrewing a third of its length from the rest. Then he halved the lower two-thirds with the same unscrewing action. He pushed the dismantled shovel under the hem of the hammer cloth drape to stow it beneath the seat of the hearse. And withdrew from the same storage compartment a four foot high wooden cross.

'Hey, I'd like a stone marker,' the Texan said suddenly. 'I'll pay extra –'

'No need,' Gold cut in. 'This is just temporary. Casket took a long time to make. I was starting in on the headstone when you came back to town today.'

'Much obliged.'

He turned his back to go over to where the obedient stallion waited: as Barnaby Gold leaned the wooden

46

cross against the front wheel of the hearse and reached again into the draped space under the seat.

'Hey, you forgot something. You don't know what name to . . . '

He had a booted foot in the stirrup and turned just his head. But what he saw caused him to withdraw the foot and turn slowly all the way around: as his voice trailed away. With the expression of mild satisfaction at having discovered something Gold had forgotten taking on a frozen quality.

What he saw across eight feet of sunlit afternoon air which suddenly felt ice-cold was Barnaby Gold aiming a gun at him. A hammerless Murcott double barrel shotgun, levelled from the right hip: the young undertaker's left hand cupped under the barrels so that the muzzles maintained a rock-steady bead on the Texan's belly.

After the initial freezing shock of the unexpected sight, Floyd Channon's features altered into a scowl and he made a motion with his right hand toward the butt of his holstered Remington.

Gold squeezed the forward trigger of the Murcott. And the cartridge exploded its load from the left hand barrel in a rapidly broadening pattern of shot. The Texan's fingers had not touched the butt of his revolver before he felt the force of countless grains of metal rip through his shirt and pants to smash into the flesh of his belly, chest and thighs.

The stallion was peppered by the outer crescents of the pattern, snorted and wheeled away. So offered no support for the falling form of Floyd Channon. Who hit the ground on his back in a billow of dust and clawed with both hands at the blood-oozing wounds in his flesh.

'Why, you murdering sonofabitch?' he screamed through his agony as Barnaby Gold advanced from the hearse and stood, splay-legged over him.

47

'Why did you pick Fairfax to make arrangements for her burial?' the undertaker asked, his finger curled to the rear trigger as he held the acrid-smelling twin muzzles of the shotgun three inches above the centre of the Texan's face.

'It was the closest place to where I killed her, frig it! I wanted her buried decent! I loved her! There were some good times! I owed her that much!' He uttered a groan, part pain, part despair. 'Why you done ...'

The undertaker squeezed the second trigger. And the Texan took the full force of the whole pattern of shot in his head. At just a fraction less than muzzle velocity. So that the skin was shredded, the tissue beneath pulped, the eyes exploded and the front of the skull was momentarily exposed – before more blood bubbled up to obscure the whiteness uncovered by the myriad droplets that sprayed to all sides in the shock wave.

Running feet hit the street and voices were raised in the tone of fearful questions. Those at the front came to an abrupt halt between the church and the house and soon a large, utterly silent throng was standing there. Watching the equally silent, deliberately moving figure of the lanky, black-clad undertaker.

He swung away from the shot-shattered corpse and went to the hearse. Returned the Murcott under the seat, lifted the wooden cross and went out into the cemetery. It required little effort to push the stem of the cross into the soil at the head of the new grave. Only then did he look up to acknowledge that he was aware of his stunned audience.

'Appreciate it if somebody would take care of the horse!' he called.

The black stallion had managed to bolt only forty feet away from the hearse, then collapsed on to his side in the slow-running stream. Where he now lay, staining the water with his blood as he screwed his head around, teeth bared as he tried to bite out the many fragments of shot sunk into his side.

Because it was a gunshot that had brought them running to the cemetery, many of the men had snatched up weapons before leaving what had occupied them. It was the blacksmith, who also acted as an unqualified vet in Fairfax, who broke away from the crowd to do Gold's bidding. He examined the multiple wounds for just a few moments: before pressing the muzzle of an old Starr .44 revolver to the head of the animal. And squeezing the trigger to end the stallion's suffering.

'Appreciate it, Mr Hogg,' the undertaker called, and removed his hat as he looked down for perhaps a full ten seconds at the neatly painted legend on the smoothly planed and perfectly jointed wood of the cross.

The years of birth and death on the upright with, along the cross member: *Emily Jane – Once beloved wife of Barnaby Gold Junior.*

CHAPTER SIX

ON his way back to rejoin the throng at the corner of the church, the powerfully built and bitterly frowning John Hogg came closer to the new grave than when he passed it to shoot the injured horse. Close enough to read what was painted on the wooden cross.

He pulled up short and expressed a greater degree of shock than when he first saw the gunshot remains of the Texan.

'Jesus, son,' he rasped.

And was ignored by the lanky young man who now swung away from the grave to stride quickly toward the hearse. Where, as he climbed up on to the cloth-draped seat, Jack Cater called: 'You ain't gonna just leave him like he is, Barnaby?'

Gold unhitched the reins from around the brake lever and replied: 'I'll take care of it,' before setting the team moving, to bring them and the hearse into a tight turn.

The bystanders, some still suffering from shock, others puzzled, some bewildered and a few angry, fell back into two groups so the rig could be driven between them.

'Somethin' you folks should know!' John Hogg yelled. 'Come on over and look see!'

The undertaker did not look back as the crowd advanced into the cemetery to join the blacksmith at the graveside, all swinging wide of the sprawled body of Floyd Channon, where a swarm of flies was gorging on the rapidly drying blood of the ghastly wounds.

There were just a handful of women in the cemetery. Most had remained in the safety of their houses and business premises and these now peered out with tacit questions in their eyes at the man riding up on the seat of the hearse. Who did nothing to satisfy their curiosity. Halted the rig out front of the funeral parlour, climbed down and went inside. To reappear less than a minute later at the mouth of the alley, dragging a plain pine coffin, which he loaded into the rear of the glass-sided hearse. Then climbed back up on to the seat, demanded another tight turn from the team and headed toward the cemetery once more.

This as the mournful-faced men and women who had read the lettering on the cross began to come around the corner of the church.

'It's terrible, son.'

'Can understand how you feel.'

'But you shouldn't have done that to him.'

'I'm real sorry, young man.'

'Thank God your poor father was taken before this happened.'

The black-garbed driver of the hearse seemed not to hear what was being said to him: certainly made no acknowledgement of any of the remarks.

The slightly-built, neatly bearded Jack Cater was the last man to appear between the church and the house. And forced himself to be heard after moving into the path of the team so that the horses had to be reined in.

'You're in big trouble, son,' he said grimly. 'After you done with the new buryin', advise you to listen to what I gotta tell you. And do what I say.'

'Soon as I'm through, plan on leaving for Europe, Mr Cater. Appreciate it if you'd stand aside.'

The town barber complied, shaking his head and muttering: 'You're a strange one and no mistake, son.'

Gold drove out to the side of the now deserted cemetery and after he had halted the hearse he remained on the seat. Shoulders hunched, head bowed and hands clasped tightly together. The attitude was one of prayer, but this was coincidental. The young undertaker held this posture for so long to keep from shaking: fighting desperately against the threat of a trembling fit that was abruptly on the point of attacking every muscle in his body.

It was a delayed reaction to a double shock. The first when he unwrapped the blanket and saw that the stinking remains were those of Emily Jane. The second when he carried out his decision – impulsively made on recognising his wife – to kill her murderer. The latter more shattering than the former because Barnaby Gold Junior had never before killed anything larger than a quail.

He overcame the desire to shake from head to toe, but the effort this required left him drained and weak. So that he almost fell when he climbed down from the seat. He leaned against a wheel and stared fixedly out at the horizon. Waited until the meeting of sky and land ceased to tilt from side to side. Then took a tin case of slim cheroots from an inside pocket of his frock coat, struck a match on the wheel rim and lit the tobacco.

The smoke negated the taste of bile in his throat and his body seemed to draw strength from it when it filled his lungs. It was only half finished, its remains squashed flat under a boot heel, when he felt ready to do what was necessary.

He dragged the pine box from the rear of the hearse and across to where the fly-covered body of Floyd Channon lay. The lid was only tacked to the sides and there was a hammer and bag of nails in the cotton sheet-lined interior.

Before he placed the faceless corpse in the coffin, he searched the pockets which were empty except for the fat roll of bills. He arranged the body with the hands clasped on the chest, then nailed down the lid.

He put the money under the seat of the hearse from where he took the three pieces of the shovel and screwed them together. Then began to dig a grave on the edge of the cemetery, just a few feet from where the plain coffin rested.

The grave, like the box, had to be longer than usual to accommodate the taller than average Floyd Channon. Barnaby Gold dug it with the easy skill of long experience. But then had to struggle, singlehanded, to get the coffin into the grave: determined the Texan without a face should have his eternal rest on his back. And the only way to achieve this was to stand the coffin on end at the foot of the grave – tip it off the edge.

It was an irreverent method of committing a corpse to the earth, but after the crash of impact and the clearing of the dust it raised, Barnaby Gold saw it had worked well enough.

He shovelled the dirt to refill the grave and when he was through the afternoon had run its course: with darkness gathering on the eastern horizon, waiting for the redness of the setting sun to fade in the west. And the smoke of many cooking fires was strong in the cooling air of dusk.

Apart from when he asked John Hogg to end the agony of the horse and was forced to listen to the ominous warning of Jack Cater, Barnaby Gold had been detached from everything that did not immediately concern him since he fired the first shot at Floyd Channon. And he remained so now, as he unscrewed the three parts of the shovel, stowed them in the accustomed place and climbed up on to the seat of the hearse.

Until he drove the rig back on to the street and saw that one of the fires pouring smoke into the evening air was not for cooking.

A building was ablaze, midway along the western side of the street: the leaping flames holding back the encroaching darkness and illuminating the entire male population of Fairfax. Who were split into three groups.

It was the funeral parlour that was being consumed by flames: burning with a ferocity that suggested they were being fuelled by more than merely the timber and fabric of the building's construction and furnishings.

And as Gold drove closer, he smelled kerosene. At the same time, he noticed that the two smaller groups of men, gathered out front of the draper's and the laundry which flanked the blazing building, were holding pails of water. Ready to douse the neighbouring premises should flying sparks threaten to set them alight, too.

The larger body of men were gathered out front of the saloon. Some of them still toting rifles or with revolvers stuck into their belts from when they had run to the cemetery earlier in the day.

Gold angled the hearse toward the saloon, but halted it short of the waiting men: to keep the fire-scared team out of range of the intense heat radiating from the burning building.

The Reverend Baxter, John Hogg, Jack Cater, Jeb Stone who owned the saloon and Festus Norbert the banker detached themselves from the large group and came toward the stalled rig.

The flickering firelight showed the grimness of their

expressions. Also illuminated the quizzical look on the youthful face of the undertaker who remained up on the seat.

'It was my idea, son,' Cater admitted as the five men stopped beside the hearse. Of these, only the blacksmith was armed with the handgun he had used to kill the wounded stallion.

'But it didn't take much to convince the whole town it was a good one,' Hogg added.

'For the good of the town, Barnaby,' the elderly preacher said.

'Mr Norbert,' Jeb Stone urged from the side of his mouth and nudged the banker with an elbow.

The bald-headed, round-faced man who was as nervous as the saloon keeper, cleared his throat and held out a paper sack that was bulky but light.

He cleared his throat. 'Everyone chipped in, young man. Not near enough to cover the market value of the property and its contents and the goodwill of the business. But there's better than three hundred dollars taken up.'

'Token of how bad we feel about what it has been necessary to do, Barnaby,' the preacher added.

While he listened to the variously anxious and embarrassed spokesman for the town, Gold took a cheroot from his case and hung it at the corner of his mouth. But he did not strike a match, leaning back to scrape it over a piece of silver trimming on the hearse, until after he had reached down to take the proffered sack of bills. Then set light to a corner of the sack before touching the flame to the tip of the cheroot. Next, as charred pieces of paper began to fall, he tossed the flaring money out on to the street.

Anger swamped Jeb Stone's nervousness and he rasped: 'Most folks have said it and most folks are right! There's somethin' just not right about you, boy!'

'Quit it, Jeb!' Cater growled. 'Once the money was given to him, it was his to do what he liked with.'

'Hey, watch him!' the saloon keeper warned. And took a step back as Gold reached under the seat of the hearse.

The others also backed off from the rig, Hogg raising a hand toward the butt of the gun stuck through his belt. He halted the move when he saw it was not the Murcott that Gold drew out from beneath the hammer cloth drape. Instead, the roll of bills he had taken from the hip pocket of Floyd Channon's pants.

'Here, Mr Norbert,' he said, extending his arm. 'Only thing of value the dead man had on him. Maybe there's some other stuff in his saddlebags. Appreciate it if you'd send the money to his family. Place called the Double-C ranch somewhere east of El Paso, Texas.'

'Sure, sure, I'll do that.' The eager-to-please banker accepted the roll.

'Won't be no need to send it, son,' John Hogg said grimly. 'After what Jack told us about the Channon family, we figure they'll come by Fairfax pretty soon.'

'The reason we burned your place, Barnaby,' the Reverend Baxter was in a hurry to explain. 'It seems the Channons of Texas are not the kind of people to allow the violent end of its son to pass unavenged. The trouble is not of our making and it was the only thing we could think to do to have proof of this when the Channons come here.'

The fire was not burning so fiercely now. There was more acrid black smoke than brightly leaping tongues of flame and the sounds of the former inferno were lessening in volume by the moment. The men with the pails of water abandoned their firewatch and crossed to join the main group before the saloon.

'We ask your forgiveness, Barnaby,' the preacher went on. 'Your father and you served this community well for the past eight years and it was a difficult decision to burn your place like we did. But we knew you were intent upon leaving Fairfax and we had to consider the welfare of those who will continue to live here.'

'All of you said your piece now?'

'Except for that advice I promised you, boy,' Jack Cater countered. 'Lot of what I've heard about the Channon clan could be rumour. But I've heard so much there just has to be more than a little truth in it. Go to Europe like you always said you wanted. But no matter where you finally light down, don't ever give up lookin' over your shoulder, boy. Reckon the United States Treasury got more money than the Channons. But I wouldn't . . .'

Barnaby Gold took up the reins and interrupted: 'I already had that message, Mr Cater. From a member of the family. Bye bye.'

'Luck to you, Barnaby.'

The team responded to a low snap of the reins and the hearse rolled forward. And the black-clad man with the smoking cheroot angled from a corner of his mouth was again immune to everything which did not affect what concerned him – driving his rig north along the street and out on to the open trail beyond.

'Crazy kid.'

'Headstrong as they come.'

'Stubborn as a damn mule.'

'City kind.' The man who rasped this spat into the dust settling behind the slow-rolling hearse.

'His Pa was from the city. And he was a fine man.'

'The finest.'

'Makes you wonder how he could father a son like that.'

57

With the fire now almost out and the departing hearse diminishing through the moonlit distance, some women were emerging on to the street.

One of them murmured sadly: 'There was nothin' wrong with the boy until that flighty Emily Jane up and took off.'

'That's what I find so hard to figure out. Why he killed that Texas feller for killin' that no good –'

'And you see what he put on the cross? *Once beloved*, that's what.'

'That Channon guy, he told Jack and me he loved Emily Jane,' Jeb Stone put in knowledgeably.

'And you know somethin' else, Jeb?' the barber said thoughtfully, as he peered out along the trail toward the receding hearse. 'Ain't the only thing them two had in common.'

'How you mean?' John Hogg asked.

'I ain't never come across two colder, one-track-minded man in all my life. And if I had to choose between the two of them, I'd have to say Barnaby Gold has the makin's of bein' the coldest.'

The storekeeper who had spat before did it again. And brought the group discussion to an end when he growled: 'As cold as all them graves he's dug.'

CHAPTER SEVEN

HAD it occurred to him to reflect upon what the people of Fairfax were talking about as he drove the hearse slowly north from town through the moonlit evening, Barnaby Gold could have made some educated guesses and come close to the kind of sentiments expressed and which man or woman spoke them.

But filling the time with such a futile mental exercise did not occur to him. Fairfax and its citizens were now just parts of his past, something he had wanted for a long time, and it was the prospect of a better future that concerned him.

And, as if in a token gesture of his firm intention to lay the past to rest, he reined the team to a halt and turned on the seat to look back down the trail. He had judged the distance correctly and expressed the ghost of a smile when he saw that Fairfax was out of sight, lost to his view beyond the line of a low rise that angled across the valley. The smile broadened, his green eyes glinting and his teeth gleaming in the moonlight. Then he took the high crowned black hat off his head, stood up and, holding it by the brim, curled his arm far back: swung it forward and released it. The hat spun away smoothly, soaring high into the air: then scaled through a long, decaying arc to bounce to the ground some thirty yards east of the trail. By which time Gold was on the seat again, folded forward and rocking with uncontrolled laughter.

Had anyone been close enough to hear and see the lanky, blond-headed young man they might have thought he was in the grip of a hysterical madness. But as it was, there were just the two black geldings in the traces of the hearse. And these animals merely turned their heads briefly to gaze dolefully at the man on the seat, then resumed their docile attitudes to await a command signal they understood.

Which came less than a minute later, when Gold's mood of unmitigated mirth was exhausted and his angularly handsome face displayed just a quiet smile of satisfaction with his lot.

This bout of body-shaking laughter was uncharacteristic of the man who now continued to drive the glass-sided rig northward. Even more alien to his nature, the people of Fairfax might have said, than his cold blooded killing of Floyd Channon. And others, who had known him before he and his father came to the tiny Arizona community eight years earlier, would have agreed.

You're a strange one and no mistake, son, Jack Cater had said to him. And, out of his hearing, another Fairfax man commented he was as cold as the graves he dug. Two opinions, expressed in countless different ways, which had been used to describe him since his childhood.

Barnaby was born in a tenement house on Pearl Street in New York's Lower East Side, the much longed-for and destined to be the only child of Barnaby and Elvira Gold, in the year of 1849. And because of the circum-

60

stances of his birth it was inevitable that he should be over-indulged to the limited extent that his mortuary attendant father and seamstress mother could afford.

The boy knew little of the harsh deprivations his parents suffered to see that he was well fed and clothed during those early years down in the Battery. For, spurred on by the needs of their child, his parents doubled and redoubled their efforts to get ahead in the world. And ahead to them meant uptown, into a decent house, with Barnaby Gold Senior working at a job that brought in enough money to support his son and allowed his wife to devote all her time to taking care of him.

They achieved the move a week after Barnaby Junior's fourth birthday: and his earliest childhood memories were centred upon a small brownstone house between Washington Square and Broadway, just around the corner from the funeral parlour where his father worked and trained to become a fully qualified mortician.

From this time on, his memory was rich with the sights and sounds and sensations of New York City, but in later years he rarely chose to resurrect the past: primarily because the images which came readily to mind were of the worst kind.

The pain-wracked dying of his mother from consumption when he was eight. The period of morose mourning, followed by a longer one of drinking and whoring, in which his father indulged. The punishment he received at the cruel hands of other children – taunts, bloodied noses, black eyes and dirtied clothing – who bullied him unmercifully because he was the son of a man who dealt in dead bodies. Then the chastisements, which caused him even greater anguish, from his father when he learned to give as good as he got. Then better than he got, so that the fights in the alleys no longer involved him.

It was at this point in his life that he could have

become as one with the society in which he was living. When, respecting his strength of character and physical courage, his contemporaries made overtures of acceptance. But, having proved himself in their eyes, he rejected their offers and became a youthful loner among those of his own age. And, much to the delight of his father, began to get better grades at the free school he attended, and show interest in the undertaking business.

Barnaby Gold Senior, sober and respectable again, had a financial investment in the funeral parlour by that time: then, upon the death of his elderly partner, became sole owner. His son was twelve and readily agreeable to terminate his education and enter the trade.

The War Between the States was hotting up at this period and although it had very little direct effect on the daily lives of Gold father and son, the newspaper reports he heard and the stories that were told him by soldiers on furlough set the man to thinking about moving out West. And the longer the fighting went on, the more convinced he became that peace, when it arrived, would be an uneasy one for a long time. With old rivalries difficult to forget in an atmosphere thick with grudges and lacking much will to forgive.

When the peace did come, Barnaby Gold Senior discovered his fears had been well-founded and that his vague idea to head out West was not exclusive to him. An exodus from the battle-ravaged East to the vastness that lay beyond the Mississippi began in earnest. And when he suggested to his seventeen-year-old son that they should join it, he expected no response other than the one which was given. An immediate if unenthusiastic acquiescence.

For this was the way of the young man.

Thus had Barnaby Gold Junior come to Fairfax, Territory of Arizona, some eight years ago – in much the same low-key manner as he had left it less than an hour earlier this very night. Only in the privacy of his own company giving more than a hint of his true feelings.

He was at the northern end of the valley in which the town was situated and the night was entering the early hours of a new day when he called a halt and made camp. Took the horses from the traces, lit a small fire, climbed into the rear of the hearse and with his frock coat rolled up to form a pillow, went to sleep between the track designed to hold a casket.

He was hungry when he fell asleep and more so for the first few seconds when he awoke. But then he saw clearly the scene that accompanied the smells of cooking food and bubbling coffee and a less mundane feeling gripped his stomach.

He had parked the hearse, hobbled the horses and lit the fire under a craggy-faced bluff to the east of the trail that ran up from the valley and across a mesa featured plateau. The sun was well risen by the time he awoke, but the immediate area was still in shade from the sixty foot high bluff. It was desert hot, though, and the three men making use of the fire to cook breakfast were stripped down to their pants, suspenders, undershirts and hose: the rest of their clothing scattered untidily on the sandy ground. Their travel-weary mounts were hitched to a mesquite tree near where the team horses were hobbled. The men sat on their saddles to one side of the freshly fuelled fire, gazing bleakly through the glass side of the hearse at the stirring Gold.

Middle-aged, unshaven, dirty faced men with tired eyes and unkempt hair: looking at the undertaker in the back of the hearse with scant interest – as if there was nothing uncommon about this situation. The man with the biggest build wore a gunbelt with a revolver in the holster. The other two had removed their gunbelts and they rested on the ground, close at hand.

None of them said anything until after Gold had pushed open the rear door with his booted feet and slid out of the hearse: was fisting the grit of sleep from his eyes.

Then: 'You rest real easy and deep, boy,' the biggest of the three opened. 'Could've done you a mischief any time in the last hour.'

'Yesterday was a heavy day,' Gold replied as he moved to go along the side of the hearse.

'Buryin' folks,' the shortest of the trio suggested.

'Two of them.'

The third man was the thinnest, with features that came close to having the set of a rodent. He directed a globule of spit into the edge of the fire.

'Know you got a double barrel shotgun hid under the seat, boy,' he said dully. 'Know you didn't trouble to eject the spent cartridges after you fired 'em. But if you made to get it, we'd have to figure as how you didn't know we knew it.'

Now, as Gold altered course to approach the fire, he grinned. It was a personable expression which, throughout his young life, had caused many people to reconsider their previously held opinions of him.

'Waking up and finding you men here like this was a shock, Mr . . . ?'

'I'm Dwyer,' the rat-faced man supplied. And nodded to the big one and the short one as he added: 'Coombs and Ketland.'

'Morning to you all. Guess I just wanted to be . . . ' He shrugged his slim shoulders. And pulled up short, fifteen feet away from the men, when Coombs pulled the Colt .45 from his holster.

'Back off, boy,' he instructed as he clicked the hammer and waved the barrel casually at Gold. 'All the way to that dead wagon. And empty out your pockets.'

The grin was abruptly gone from the good-looking face, leaving it as devoid of expression as those of the seated men.

Dwyer spat into the fire again. 'Dish out the grub, Ketland,' he said. And, in the same tone, 'Put a couple of shots into his legs, Coombs.'

Barnaby Gold recovered from the second shock and quickly backed to the rear wheel of the hearse: as the sun climbed high enough to glare down on to this area in front of the bluff.

'You're a fast learner, boy,' Coombs said as Ketland used a dipper to ladle a good smelling mixture of bacon and beans on to three plates. 'We can do you a mischief or not, dependin' on you. Makes no odds to us. Be over the border by noon and one more dead man markin' our back trail won't ... '

'Here, eat,' Ketland interrupted and thrust a plate across the sand at Coombs. Then poured out three tin mugs of coffee.

The youthful undertaker had started to empty his pockets as soon as he bumped his back against the wheel. A bunch of keys to the now destroyed funeral parlour and living quarters out back. A handkerchief. A comb. Matches. Forty-five cents in coins. And nineteen hundred and six dollars, comprising the fee Floyd Channon had paid for Emily Jane's funeral plus the sum total of liquid capital in the Barnaby Gold and Son business.

Only when the roll of bills was dropped to the ground among the trivia did the three men curtail their eating.

'Hot damn, that looks a lot!' Ketland said.

'It ain't tobacco money, that's for sure,' Coombs agreed.

Dwyer finished chewing a mouthful of food, swallowed it and asked: 'How much, boy?'

Gold told him.

'Stole?'

'Earned.'

'Seems there's a good livin' in dead folks,' Ketland said, and laughed harshly.

Dwyer ignored him. 'It's stole now.'

'Guessed it,' Gold acknowledged.

'Go get it, Ketland.'

The short man was eager to comply with the order: tipped what was left of his breakfast on to the ground and got to his feet. Was careful not to get into the line of fire from Coombs' gun as he claimed the money and returned to the fireside. And showed scowling reluctance for just a moment before he surrendered the roll into Dwyer's outstretched hand. This as the sun shed its glaring light on the area of the fire.

Dwyer put the money into his hip pocket and went on eating.

Coombs asked: 'This trail ends at a place called Fairfax. You know it?'

'I've just left there.'

'No telegraph line to there, seems?'

'That's right.'

'Got a lawman there?'

'No.'

Coombs looked at Dwyer. 'Sounds good, don't it?'

Dwyer remained as unimpressed as ever. And directed some bean-coloured saliva into the fire. 'Just one thing I don't like.'

'What's that?'

'The boy give up the money too easy.'

'Shit, you said for Coombs to blast his legs from under him if he didn't do what he was told,' Ketland reminded.

66

'Go check out the rig. Includin' that coat he was sleep-in' on. Maybe he's just shit scared. Or maybe he tossed us peanuts hopin' we wouldn't figure to look for the real bundle.'

He did not shift the stare of his wearied eyes away from the expressionless face of Barnaby Gold as he spoke.

'I reckon it's a waste of friggin' time,' Ketland complained.

'You're through eatin'. Me and Coombs ain't yet. So you got time on your hands.'

Ketland said: 'Shit,' and got to his feet again. But with less enthusiasm this time. And he stooped to slide the Colt from his holster on the ground before heading for the rear of the hearse. He carried it low at his side and paid more attention to Coombs' gun – making sure that, as before, he did not get between it and the black-clad youngster.

'Why'd you bother with a fire, boy?' Dwyer asked.

'Uh?' Gold grunted, after watching Ketland go to the open rear door of the hearse and reach inside.

'The fire? Why'd you want a fire? We checked while you were sleepin' like a baby. You're travellin' light. No grub, no shavin' gear, no friggin' nothing'.'

Ketland drew out the frock coat and patted the pockets. Found only the tin box of cheroots, which he claimed.

'Keep warm. But turned out I was so dead beat all I could do was climb into the rig and sleep.'

Ketland began to tap his fist on the floor of the hearse, searching for a hidden compartment that would be revealed by a hollow sound.

'Crazy thing to do in country like this, boy. Go to sleep with a fire blazin' like a friggin' beacon. With a gun that ain't loaded and is way outta reach anyway.'

'Town folks, I figure,' Coombs said as both men

finished eating. 'Greenhorn outside of where the side-walks end.'

Dwyer ignored him, as Ketland transferred his attention to the space beneath the hammer cloth covered seat of the hearse – going around the far side of the vehicle from where Gold stood.

'Where you headed?'

'Europe.'

'Shit, you didn't make it too far,' Coombs muttered.

Dwyer tossed the dregs from his coffee mug on to the fire. 'If it hadn't been us, boy, it'd have been some others. Way you are.'

Gold shrugged his narrow shoulders. 'Just wasn't thinking straight, I guess. Like I said, it was a heavy day.'

'Ain't nothin' aboard but nothin',' Ketland reported.

'See if he ain't wearin' a money belt or got some fancy secret pocket in his pants.' Dwyer obviously did not think there was much chance of this. 'And don't hog them there cheroots. Toss them over.'

Ketland rasped: 'Shit,' again and scaled the tin box toward the fire.

'Way I see it,' the rat-faced man growled, 'a boy like you didn't oughta be allowed out on his own. Let alone smoke.'

He flipped open the lid, took a cheroot for himself and handed the box to Coombs. Then reached to lift a glowing stick from the edge of the fire.

Ketland, angrily resentful of doing the chores while his two partners took their ease, waved his gun at Gold to order the young undertaker away from the wheel of the hearse.

In expression and attitude, Gold appeared resigned to obey whatever order was given him as he stepped forward two paces, so that Ketland could move behind him.

'Hands out to your sides, boy.'

Gold extended both his arms to their fullest limit, straight out from his shoulders: as he felt the pressure of the Colt muzzle against the base of his spine.

Dwyer's cheroot was alight and the first taste of its smoke was being relished with a sigh and a grin of pleasure.

Coombs was searching the fire for a suitable stick to light the one he had taken from the box.

Ketland kept the Colt muzzle tight to Gold's back as he used his free hand to pat the left side of the under-taker's pants. Then the gun moved fractionally as he awkwardly crossed one arm over the other to make a cursory exploration of the other pants leg.

Which was when Barnaby Gold whirled. To swing around anti-clockwise in what for a second looked like some clumsily executed ballet movement – as he dipped to the left with both arms still fully extended to the sides. Then his left arm came down and back very fast, the wrist twisted and the hand clawed. To clasp the barrel of the Colt and force it to aim at the ground. This as he flung his right arm ahead of the body turn, bending the elbow and the fingers of the hand.

'Shit!' Ketland screamed, the word venting from his throat at the same instant that the Colt exploded a shot into the ground. And Gold's right hand took a grip on the nape of his neck.

For just part of another second, Gold had his back to the men at the side of the fire. But before that same second had run its course, the full three hundred and sixty degree turn was completed. And the short of stature Ketland was stumbling toward his partners, on the verge of pitching headlong to the ground, as a result of the violent thrust of Gold's right hand against his neck. While the black-clad youngster was in possession of the Colt – uncocked, holding it around the barrel in his left

69

hand after wrenching it from Ketland's grip.

'Blast the bastard!' Dwyer shrieked, spitting out the cheroot and hurling himself to the side, both hands reaching for the gun in the holster on the ground.

Coombs hurled away the stick with a glowing end and kept the freshly lit cheroot clamped between his teeth as he strove to get his bulky frame up off the ground: seeking a clear shot at Gold over the tumbling form of Ketland.

Gold dropped on to his haunches and tipped himself to the left. The Colt was in both his hands now, the hammer cocked. He squeezed the trigger with the index finger of his right hand. And clicked back the hammer with his left thumb.

Two reports sounded, the second a sliver of time after the first. He heard a bullet thud into the timber of the hearse. Saw blood on the undershirt of Coombs as the big man's scowl changed to a look of surprise.

Ketland was sprawled face down on the ground by now and he was wailing like a baby.

Coombs looked down at the bloodstain spreading across his filthy undershirt, then dropped his gun and tipped over backwards.

'You sneaky sonofa –'

From where he lay, full-length on his side, Barnaby Gold tracked the Colt away from the dying man, over the prone form of the crying one and halted its move when it was aimed at the shouting one. Who was just as angry at himself as at Gold – because of his clumsiness as he snatched up his gunbelt, and struggled to unfasten the thong that held the revolver in the holster.

Dwyer was halfway to his feet, and the second bullet exploded from the gun in Gold's double-handed grip, cracked between the legs of the rat-faced man as he came erect. And made to aim his own gun while it was still in the holster, attached to the bullet-heavy gunbelt.

Ketland began to beat at the ground with the heels of his fists, the sight and sound of him even more baby-like.

Gold thumbed back the hammer, tilted the gun and squeezed the trigger.

Dwyer took the bullet in the chest and swayed back, then forward. He merely grunted. Then was hit in the chest again. He was forced to take a backward step, struggled to stay erect. But the life ran out of him through the two holes in his flesh. He dropped his gunbelt, the death rattle sounded in his throat and he fell like a sawn tree. Into the fire that sprayed up sparks and ash amid the billowing smoke around his body. Then flames tongued at his clothing, which flared to sear him naked and blacken his unfeeling flesh.

'Dear God in Heaven, save me! I know I been wicked! I done wrong things all my life! Ma! Pa! Mister, please don't!'

Gold was back on his feet, gazing morosely at the fire as the flames died and made sizzling sounds while reducing Dwyer's body moisture to steam: aware that the bills the man had put into his hip pocket were now black flecks among the ashes.

He went forward, intent upon grasping one of the unburnt feet and dragging the partially cremated body from the fire.

It was then that the terrified Ketland began his tearful pleas to the Almighty, his parents and Barnaby Gold. And it was as if the dejected young undertaker had for-gotten about the survivor of the trio until now. For he interrupted his advance, alongside the man, and looked down at the face which was in profile. Pressed to the ground that was damp with his sweat and tears. Grains of

71

sand were disturbed by expelled breath as he completed his entreaty.

'Please don't kill me, mister.'

The Colt was held in just the right hand now, as the hammer was cocked.

Ketland craned his neck around to stare up in horror at the aimed gun and the face etched with bitterness of the man who held it.

'You cold-hearted . . . nnnnoooo . . . ! '

A fifth bullet blasted from the muzzle of the Colt. Cracked almost vertically downward for less than three feet and drilled into Ketland's temple. The head was slammed back to the ground by the force of the impact and now blood dripped to mix with the sweat and tears in the sand.

Barnaby Gold let out a breath in a low, whistling, sigh. Dropped the gun and continued on toward the fire to do what he had intended.

Then he stood for a full minute in the heat and glare of the morning sun, as the desert flies zoomed in to feast on the blood of the newly dead. But the expected fit of shaking that had attacked him in the wake of his killing of Floyd Channon did not materialise.

And he grunted his approval of this, went to the hearse, drew the sections of the shovel from under the seat and slowly screwed them together. Then dug a four foot deep communal grave, arranged the three bodies decorously in its bottom and shovelled back the displaced sand.

Still he experienced no reaction to the multiple shootings and the period of high tension that had preceded the explosion of violence.

He dismantled the shovel and replaced it beneath the seat. Retrieved the belongings that he had been forced to drop to the ground beside the hearse, and the tin box which now contained just two cheroots. Next freed the dead men's mounts from the mesquite and put the team horses in the traces.

All he took that was not his was a battered and sweat-stained roll brimmed, low crowned Stetson. It was the only one of the three that fitted him and just happened to be black, like the rest of his clothing. Then he climbed aboard the hearse and set it rolling, a freshly lit cheroot angled from the corner of his mouth.

By this time the three saddle horses had wandered off in search of grazing and water. And the fire was just a heap of grey ashes surrounded by saddles, bedrolls, items of foodstuff and clothing and the overturned cooking and coffee pots: discarded plates and mugs.

And the desert flies, denied their breakfast of blood, were turning their voracious attention to the greasy remains of bacon and beans in the pot and on the plates.

Soon they would swarm away and later – maybe today or maybe not – someone travelling the trail would find the abandoned camp and its paraphernalia. By which time the elements could well have disguised the grave under the bluff and obliterated the signs which the hearse left in its wake. In which event the mystery of why three men had apparently left the campsite in such seeming haste was likely never to be solved.

Whereas, if the grave was discovered and the citizens of Fairfax learned of it . . . ? Many would be eager to expound the suspicions they had long held about a former member of their community. Their wagging tongues providing the verbal mortar to form the foundation of a reputation.

Such ponderings on what might or might not be the result of the triple killings did not enter the mind of Barnaby Gold as he drove the hearse slowly north along the trail. And neither did he indulge in embittered regret at having lost all his money, except for forty-five cents.

73

He was damned hungry again, and scowled because of his failure to realise that this was the way it would be – when he was back at the camp under the bluff where there were three saddles hung with bags bulging with supplies.

Knew he would have to put his aim of getting to Europe at the back of his mind. Devote more attention to his needs for the immediate future.

CHAPTER EIGHT

COOMBS' sardonic comment that Barnaby Gold was a fast learner hit the nail squarely on the head.

On his mother's knee, in the school room and alongside his father in the workshop and at the cold slab, the youngster had been quick to pick up the rudiments of living, the fundamentals of an education and the skills of the undertaking trade.

But the lessons which had stood him in good stead in dealing with Floyd Channon, the citizens of Fairfax and Dwyer, Coombs and Ketland were not so formalised. Were learned out on the mean streets of New York City.

For a long time after he was of an age and had developed the inclination to go outside the confines of the bounds his mother would have preferred to keep him within, he either took his knocks without retaliation or he went far out of his way to avoid confrontation with his tormentors.

So it was that he soon became known not only as the kid whose father robbed poor widows, but also a yellow coward. Until a cold winter's evening shortly after his father had buried his mother. When he saw his father thrown out of a known brothel and collapse into a drunken stupor in the slush-filled gutter. And three of his classmates came by as he was weepingly attempting to revive his father.

For maybe a full minute sought to ignore the taunts they hurled at him along with the icy hard snowballs. And then it was as if one of the tight packed balls that hit his head upset some delicately balanced mechanism which controlled his character.

He whirled, rose and lunged. All three of his fellow eight-year-olds were stunned with surprise. He head-butted one in the belly and saw vomit spew from the boy's mouth as he swung to face the other two. One of these he kicked in the crotch as the other turned to run away, his scream of terror louder than the sounds of pain from the injured kids.

But he lost his footing on the slippery sidewalk and Barnaby Gold was on him in an instant: kneeling on the small of his back, hands fastened around his neck and banging his forehead on the ice-sheened cement. And might well have killed his victim had not two patrolmen come slithering around a corner in response to the screams.

Late that night, after he was sobered up sufficiently to understand the patrolmen's version of events, Barnaby Gold Senior took off his belt and beat his son's rear until the flesh bled.

The following day and for a few more, the other children at school eyed the tall and skinny son of the undertaker with curiosity instead of the usual scorn. While Barnaby Gold himself nursed resentment toward his father and remained detached from the new situation in which he found himself. Until the school bully, two years Gold's elder and of matching height but with a weight advantage, was goaded into putting the boy's new-found reputation to the test. To see if he had simply got very lucky very quickly.

Every kid in the school except for Barnaby Gold knew what was afoot. So he alone was surprised when the older boy stepped out from behind a pile of rubble on the vacant lot which was on his route between school and home. Then, within moments of the tacit challenge being made, almost every other pupil who knew there was to be a fight converged on the lot to watch it.

Yellow was something Barnaby Gold had never been. The reason he had tried to avoid fights or been passive in taking his punishment before the recent incident was that he did not consider himself good at whatever skills were necessary to knock an assailant so hard to the ground that he either couldn't or wouldn't get up again. And it was a characteristic of him, even at such a tender age, to dislike doing anything at which he did not excel.

To a tumultuous cheer, the bigger and older boy came in with fists clenched: in a juvenile imitation of an orthodox fighter's style. And Barnaby Gold put into practise the lessons he had subconsciously learned in dealing with the three aggressors a few evenings ago. Mixed in with some points he had picked up by always previously being on the receiving end of the punishment.

He remained passive until the first roundhouse punch was flung toward him. Then sprang the surprise. By bobbing under the punch and thudding a knee into the other boy's crotch.

The injured boy, shocked by the sudden switch from inaction to counterattack, dropped both hands to the source of his pain and bent double.

Angry accusations of dirty fighting were shrieked at Barnaby Gold. Who ignored them as he took hold of his challenger's curly hair in both hands and used his knee again – to smash it into the pain-contorted face and start blood flowing from the nostrils.

Against the three boys he had been in the grip of a glowing hot rage. But by instinct he had assaulted those parts of their anatomy where he had been hurt most when he was attacked. This time he was starkly aware of what he was doing and why he was doing it. He had no wish to toy with a superior enemy and nor did he seek self-gratification or acclaim from the audience by emerging the winner. He simply wanted to get it over with and go home. As soon as possible.

He let go of the mop of hair and the school bully fell over on to his back, then rolled on to his side and curled up into a ball, groaning his agony and humiliation.

Barnaby Gold started to move away. The boy on the ground was able to muster the strength to subdue his pain and hurl a handful of mud at the son of the under-taker. As unemotionally as before, Gold stopped, turned and made to launch a vicious kick at his kidneys. But a burly streetcar driver on his way to work on the evening shift stepped forward to prevent this.

And, without a word, Barnaby Gold went home. To endure another beating from his whiskey-smelling father who saw the mud-splattered jacket and bloodstained pants as signs of a fight.

It was the last belting he ever received, for there were no more fights involving the boy who – had he been so inclined – could easily have become the new school bully or the most popular pupil. For in the cold winter light of the following days those who had witnessed the short-lived showdown on the vacant lot came to admire the way Gold had handled the situation and respect him for not taking advantage of his victory.

He had fought dirty, sure. But when the chips were down and the odds were heavily loaded it was the only way to fight. The fact that, without adult intervention, he might have smashed one boy's face to a pulp and done serious internal damage to the vital organs of another . . . ?

It was early evening when the former undertaker of Fairfax drove his hearse into the town of Standing: he weak from hunger and the horses close to exhaustion from the long haul through the heat of the day.

Standing was about four times as large as Fairfax: an older community which had started out as a mission, then an army post – both now defunct. It had a mixed American and Mexican population, many of whom worked at a company owned silver mine and ore crushing plant to the west of the three-street town.

It was supper time and most people were eating behind doors, which were closed against the first chill of the night air when the hearse rolled down Main Street. And among those who did see it, it was cause for only passing comments for both the Gold father and son had driven the rig to Standing on several previous occasions.

The smell of food mingling with the woodsmoke from so many stovepipes made the hunger pangs in Gold's stomach almost painful. But with just forty-five cents in his pocket, he drove on by the Mexican cantina that served meals and the restaurant a few doors along the street. Did not rein the team to a halt until after he had steered the rig around the corner on to Silver Mine Road: climbed down from the seat out front of Ward's Funeral Parlour which was on the very edge of town. Where the open trail started to curve toward the canyon from which the ore was mined.

The single storey adobe building was in darkness, but a dim light showed at the draped window of the small frame house in a grove of Alligator Junipers out back. Barnaby Gold hand-brushed trail dust off his clothing as he went along the well trodden pathway that led around the side of the parlour, across a yard on which an elderly and worse for wear hearse was parked, timber planks and ready-made coffins were stacked and a partially inscribed headstone lay, then through the twenty foot high trees.

At the door beside the lighted window, he curtailed his intention to rap the knuckles of a fist on the panel. For the window was not quite closed at the bottom and through the gap came the sound of a woman giggling.

Then: 'I think you have had a little more to drink than you should have, *Señor* Ward.'

A man laughed. 'Reckon that means you gotta work harder for your money, Maria.'

'*Si*. I think so, too. But can I have a drink, too?'

'It ain't no bottle neck I want you to suck.' There was a commanding harshness in his tone. Then another laugh. 'Hey, don't you look so friggin' sullen, woman. I got an idea.' There was the sound of liquid gurgling from a bottle. But not into a glass. 'Here, try that. Special kinda cocktail, maybe?'

He laughed longer and louder but in a while this sound died away to be replaced by others. Uttered by both the Standing undertaker and the Mexican whore.

Barnaby Gold clicked his tongue against the roof of his mouth and moved away from the house, to lean against the trunk of a tree and light his final cheroot. The sounds of the whore's false passion and of Clay Ward's struggle to overcome the effects of liquor so that his lust could be released reached the black-clad young man at a muted volume. But no conjured up images of the scene inside the house entered his mind to stir a desire of his own. His stomach rumbled its emptiness and the tobacco smoke scorched the membranes of his throat.

Crickets chirped and bats beat their wings. A player piano began to sound the notes of *Dixie* from the Silver Lode Saloon halfway along Main Street.

Barnaby Gold displayed the same brand of stoic patience as had Floyd Channon.

'Get away from me!' The sharp sound of flesh striking flesh and a strangled scream accompanied Clay Ward's snarled words. 'Call yourself a friggin' whore? A twelve-year-old unbroke girl could suck better than you!'

Another cry of pain and a heavy thud, as if the woman had been pushed hard to the floor.

'But *Señor* Ward, I am not to blame for what the whiskey has – '

'Get outta my house! And tell that old bag that owns you whores, the next time I ask for a woman, I wanna woman! Not some titless, fat-assed . . . '

'But I am not dressed, *señor!*'

'I don't give a frig if you gotta walk bare-assed naked from here to Tucson! Get outta here, damn you!'

Bare feet slapped the floor, moving fast. Gold pushed his back away from the deeply furrowed, alligator-skin-like bark of the tree and moved out of the shade into the bright moonlight. This as the door of the house was jerked open and Maria emerged, seemingly thrust into the night by a physical force as if each obscenity hurled at her by Ward was a shove against her back. Her slim, long legged, light brown skinned body was naked and she was clutching a dress and a pair of shoes. Her pretty, thirty-year-old face was wet with tears and a bruise was already starting to show on her right cheek.

She was brought up sharply with a gasp of fear by the sight of Gold on the pathway. Then she recognised him and pleaded: 'Barnaby?'

'Hello, Maria,' he said dully as he stepped aside to go around her. 'Bye bye.'

She spat a Spanish curse and ran into the deep shade under a tree to get dressed as Gold, the cheroot clamped between his teeth again, entered the house and closed the door at his back.

Clay Ward was still seated in the deep armchair where the whore had done her best for him and failed. He was muttering now, as he fastened the front of his pants. Stopped and looked up at the sound of the door closing, to squint angrily at his visitor through the dim light of a single kerosene lamp turned to a low wick.

'Who's that?' he slurred.

Gold crossed to a centrally placed table in the small parlour and adjusted the wick of the lamp. The brighter light showed a poorly furnished, untidy and unclean room. Into which the Standing undertaker fitted well.

He was fifty years old, short and painfully thin. With an almost skeletonal face, the deeply wrinkled skin of which fell loosely from the cheekbones and jawlines. Above the face was a mop of greasy black hair that hung down to cover his ears at either side. He was dressed in longjohns and baggy pants, his ugly feet bare.

'Ah, the Gold boy,' he said after a long, squint-eyed look at the black frock-coated man in the brighter level of light. He picked up a half empty bottle of rye from the floor beside the chair. 'Whores ain't what they used to be. How's your Pa, boy?'

'Like whores, Mr Ward. He's dead.'

The older man did not pause in drinking from the bottle until he had his fill. Then: 'Well, I'll be. Peaceful end was it?'

'Had one of his coughing fits. Then a heart seizure. The rig's out on the street.'

'What's that?'

82

'The hearse you were always eager to buy. It's outside.'

Clay Ward seemed suddenly sober. 'Why's that, boy?'

'I'm out of the undertaking business. Going to Europe.'

Ward rose from the armchair with a creak of bones. 'It's what you always said you wanted to do, after that pretty young wife of yours run off.'

A nod. 'Just like you always wanted to buy the circular hearse, Mr Ward. As I recall, your last offer was five hundred dollars.'

'That it was. To you and your Pa both, over to the Silver Lode. Let's go take another look at her.'

He led the way out of the house. The player piano in the distant saloon was striking out with *Home on the Range*. Ward still carried the whiskey bottle.

'Why just the hearse, boy?'

'I'll sell the team, too.'

'I already got a team serves my purpose. It's the hearse appeals to me. But seein' as how you're givin' up the entire business over to Fairfax – '

'The parlour and all that was in it got burned out, Mr Ward.'

'Well, I'll be. That's a damn shame, boy. So there ain't no undertakin' facilities over in Fairfax now?'

They emerged from the side of the Standing parlour on to the end of Silver Mine Road. Where the travel-wearied horses stood disconsolately in the traces of the dust-covered hearse.

'Guess the folks there would be happy to have you take over, Mr Ward.'

'Reckon I can oblige them, boy.'

He walked along one side of the hearse, around the rear and down the other side. And with his fingertips touched the glass panels and the polished timber, felt the hammer cloth drape over the seat and explored the silver trim here and there. Occasionally sucked from the bottle.

Then: 'What's this here, boy?'

Barnaby Gold ground out the cheroot under a boot heel before going to look at what had caused Ward to pause. Saw where a large splinter of black painted wood had been blasted from a panel by the shot from Coombs' Colt.

'Can be fixed in no time, I'd say.'

Ward spat. 'Reckon so. Two fifty bucks.'

'Say that again.'

'You heard, boy.'

'Because of that scratch?'

'No, boy. Not on account of the damage. Matter of business in the marketplace. Made that offer of five hundred when I was itchin' to buy and your Pa was in no mind to sell. Way it is now, I still want her. And you're real eager to sell her. With no other customer closer than Tucson interested in makin' a deal.'

The younger man considered what was said by the older one for long moments, his good-looking face wearing a scowl of dislike. Then he nodded.

'Okay, Mr Ward. We have a deal. You want to go bring the money?'

The Standing undertaker grinned, displaying blackened teeth. 'Sure thing, boy. Real glad you understand the situation.'

He hurried back along the pathway, as if anxious to complete the transaction in case Gold was tempted to back out. But Gold had no intention of doing this. Continued to scowl as he took the team from the traces and then got the Murcott shotgun and the three pieces of the shovel from beneath the seat. He had expected Clay Ward to do some hard bargaining, for the man was known as much for his closeness with money as for his drunkenness and lechery. But he had not thought to get so little for what was probably the most impressive hearse in the territory.

Then, minus the bottle and breathless from hurrying, the man was back, a stack of bills in his hand.

'There you go, boy. Count it if you've a mind to.'

Barnaby Gold transferred the money to the pocket of his frock coat that held the empty cheroot tin. 'I've a feeling you've counted it at least twice yourself, Mr Ward.'

Now the Standing undertaker scowled his distaste for the implicit taunt about his meanness. But quickly abandoned it.

'Like to buy that neat shovel you got, too.'

'It's not for sale.'

'Why'd you want it if you ain't in the business no more?'

'Sentimental value, Mr Ward. Bye bye.'

He turned, with his burdens under one arm, holding the bridles of both black horses in the other hand. To wheel the animals and lead them back along Silver Mine Road toward the centre of town.

'Sorry to hear about your Pa, boy!' Ward called after him.

Barnaby Gold looked briefly back at him to accuse: 'You're a liar as well as a thief.'

CHAPTER NINE

THE quiet-spoken and unsmiling young man in black ate a supper of two orders of beef stew in the Main Street restaurant and then transacted some more business with Standing merchants. All of whom expressed genuine sorrow for the death of his father: but made no attempt beyond this to bridge the distance which Barnaby Gold's attitude placed between himself and those he approached.

He traded the team for a saddle-broke black gelding plus enough cash to buy a big Denver saddle and accoutrements. With a surplus to cover the cost of a week's provisions, fifty cheroots, cooking and eating utensils, a bedroll and some shaving and washing gear. But he had to draw on the money from the sale of the hearse to purchase goods and service from the elderly gunsmith.

A carton of fifty cartridges for the shotgun. And a gun-belt and attachments: a holster on the right side and a slotted plate on the left. In the low-slung holster was a Peacemaker .45 with a wooden butt. Fitted to the plate by a stud was an eagle-butt Peacemaker, the grip of mother-of-pearl and with a cutaway trigger guard.

It was a second-hand, well used rig and he bought it on impulse because at fifty dollars it seemed like a bargain. Which was what he truthfully told the gunsmith who had known him and his ways for as long as every other merchant he did business with that night.

'It's a gunslinger's rig, boy. And I ain't never thought of you as no fast draw, quick-fire artist. A bargain ain't a bargain unless a man has a use for it.'

The puzzled old timer said this with a shake of his head as he gave Gold back the Murcott after shortening the barrels and fixing a metal hook to the stockplate of the shotgun.

'Bye bye, Mr Murchison,' was all the response he received as Barnaby Gold left his store, frock coat unfastened to accommodate the bulk of the gunbelt.

When the former undertaker of Fairfax went into the barbering parlour next to the saloon for a shave, it was necessary for him to remove his necktie. And when he emerged with two days' and a night's blond bristles gone from his cheeks, jaw and throat, he left the tie behind.

The Mother Lode was doing good business now, which deterred Gold from entering through the batwings to take a couple of drinks. He had never liked crowded places. The music from the player piano had a spiritual beat to it.

A Mexican whore – young and with a fuller figure than Maria – was lounging provocatively in the arched doorway of the cantina, long hair masking half her face, body turned so that her breasts were silhouetted against the light and the hem of her dress hiked up by a hand scratching her thigh. He felt a mild stir of wanting between his legs as the girl saw him watching her: and altered the movement of her hand from a vigorous scratching to a seductive caressing.

'She's new in town, son. Doc Carradine's checked her out and says she's clean.'

The man who made the recommendation emerged from the saloon batwings: the star on the left side of his sheepskin coat glinting in the light.

Sheriff Walt Glazer was sixty. Old for a lawman, but Standing was a law-abiding town to the extent that the office of sheriff was virtually an honorary one. He was tall and heavy, with a fleshy face and a belly that overhung his belt. He had given up tobacco a year since, but was hardly ever seen without a big-bowled pipe angled from one side of his wide mouth.

'Guess I'll pass it up.'

Glazer leaned against a support of the saloon's stoop roof. 'Forever that'll be. Word is you're headed for Europe.'

'Right, Sheriff.'

'Expectin' trouble over there?'

'Uh?'

'Packin' two guns. One of them hung on a quick-fire device.'

'Right, Sheriff.'

The whore spat sullenly into the street and withdrew across the threshold of the cantina.

'Never seen you tote any gun except for that Murcott. And that when we was out huntin'.'

'Appreciate your concern, Sheriff.'

His newly purchased black gelding was hitched to the saloon rail, the shotgun hung from the right front rigging ring of the saddle and the three pieces of the shovel pushed through the centre of the bedroll. He swung up astride the horse.

'Been trouble already, maybe?'

'Nothing I wasn't able to handle.'

Glazer shifted the dead pipe from one side of his mouth to the other. Nodded sagely. 'I'm one that's always considered you a capable young feller, son. But down here in this piece of the country, not much ever happens a capable man can't take care of.' He waved a hand to indicate the trail that cut away north-west from the end of Main Street. 'Out there, though. A whole damn world full of all manner of trouble. You take care now. Come back to see us one day, maybe?'

Gold tugged on the reins to turn the horse away from the hitching rail. Said: 'Bye bye, Sheriff,' and trotted the gelding along the street.

He was aware that he knew little of the world which lay beyond the sandstone ridges of the Huachuca Mountains. Except for an area of a few blocks in New York City and what he had seen from the railroad car and stagecoach window on the long, arduous journey from the eastern seaboard to the south-west. But as the lights of Standing faded into the distance behind him, he made no attempt to form preconceived opinions of what to expect based upon the ominously spoken words of Walt Glazer.

He had seldom indulged in trying to forecast what the future held, be the omens good or bad. Even as a child he had never looked excitedly forward to birthdays and Christmases. Which was an attitude, so unchildlike, that used to upset – even anger – those adults who came into contact with him lacking a forewarning of his reticent and introspective character.

'He seems like a nice little feller. Kinda quiet though, Mr Gold.'

'He's always polite to folks. But cold with it, wouldn't you say?'

'Does like he's told, with no backchat. If only he didn't make it seem like he's doin' you a big favour.'

'He seems happy enough, but he don't hardly ever smile as I've seen.'

Most of the good things that were said about Barnaby

Gold Junior during his boyhood and youth were qualified with *ifs* and *buts*. Often, when it was not thought the boy or his father could overhear, bald statements about his attitudes and behaviour were made which used such words as: arrogant, vain, selfish, disdainful, supercilious and dumb insolence.

But after the need to fight was in the past and his father had drank and whored the bitterness of losing his wife out of his system, the confined world in which the boy lived came to accept him for what he was: and allowed him to plough his own furrow through it in the manner he chose.

A loner's manner that during boyhood precluded games and in adolescence kept girls at bay. There was school, then work. And in the spare time after both and the household chores, books occupied him. And long hours at the East or West Street wharves looking at the ships. Or maybe, right down on the tip of the Battery, gazing out across the harbour toward the Atlantic Ocean.

So his father was pleasantly surprised when his seventeen-year-old, apparently sea-loving son readily agreed to move out to landlocked Arizona Territory after the end of the war.

This part of the country appealed to Barnaby Gold Senior because, not only did it offer a good business opportunity, it was also reputed to have a fine climate for a man with bronchial troubles. He looked at Tucson first, then Standing. But both towns already had morticians. So the Golds came to Fairfax, the father's excitement and happiness marred only by his son's lack of enthusiasm.

And the citizens of Fairfax felt precisely the same. They needed the services of an undertaker and Barnaby Gold Senior was just the right kind of friendly, easygoing man who fitted well into the small community.

While the slow to smile, taciturn youngster made no effort to integrate himself into his new surroundings.

Thus it was like New York again in one respect – the local people finding it difficult to understand his temperament, admitting to failure and finally accepting him for what he was. Most did so quickly when his father assured them that nobody – even himself – had ever been able to enter the closed and very private world in which the youngster existed. While some of Barnaby Gold Junior's contemporaries, of both sexes, found it more difficult to come to terms with him.

With his lithe, loose-limbed build, blond hair and cool good looks allied to his polite manner and the mystery of his big city background, he was attractive to the naïve young country girls of Fairfax. Who competed to meet the unwitting challenge of his morose aloofness. Which riled the unsophisticated teenage boys who had previously been their beaux. And for the first few months after the move to Fairfax, the atmosphere wherever the town's younger set congregated had often been charged with tension – with the danger that the newcomer would again have to resort to violence to establish his right to be as he wanted to be.

But then the girls, one by one, abandoned their efforts. Some with resignation, others with an angry feeling of having been scorned. While their opposite numbers were, for the most part, content to ignore the son of the undertaker and happy that the situation was back to what it had been before he showed up in town. Thus, since there had been no backing away from fights and no fighting in which the newcomer's underlying viciousness was seen, there was no call to brand him a coward or to accuse him of foul play.

He was a strange one, that was all. Considered to have something wrong 'up top'. And 'down below', too, some giggling girls and guffawing boys maintained. But Barnaby Gold Junior waited for almost two years, taking his own time and paying no attention to external influences, before he started to visit the cantina in Standing and so exploded this myth.

When he made his second night camp away from Fairfax, Barnaby Gold lit another fire at the side of the trail: and although on this occasion he did sit at it for a while to warm himself before stretching out under the blankets of his bedroll, its prime purpose was the same as before. But even though it glowed far into the early hours of a new day, its embers and smoke attracted no unwelcome visitors.

He awoke with the first shaft of sunlight that lanced over the eastern ridges and within thirty minutes had drunk two mugs of coffee, eaten some bread and hard cheese and washed up and shaved: allowing an arc of bristles to remain along his top lip and to either side of his mouth. Then he saddled the gelding and lashed his furled bedroll on behind.

But he did not yet remove the hobble from the animal's forelegs.

The campsite was in a shallow basin under a rugged butte that towered a hundred feet high a half mile to the west. The ground surface to either side of the trail was of shale in which an occasional greasewood, saltbush, squawbush and mesquite grew. And cactus plants were established on the long slope that fell away from the base of the butte.

It was toward these that Barnaby Gold headed, coming to a halt ten feet in front of a man-high cereus with extended arms of unequal length.

He clicked his tongue against the roof of his mouth

and drew the Peacemaker from the holster. He thumbed
back the hammer, held the gun out at arm's length from
the shoulder and squeezed the trigger.

The recoil caused his arm to jerk upwards and the
bullet soared high into the air. His face expressionless, he
ignored where it came to rest and glanced over his
shoulder while the crack of the shot was still resounding
off the face of the bluff. Some hundred yards away from
him, the gelding was uneasy.

He turned, cocked the hammer of the revolver, angled
his arm downwards and fired a second shot. Saw a small
piece of cactus flesh taken out of the side of the plant by
the .45 shell.

The gelding was more distressed by the gunshot and its
echo.

The animal's new owner exploded four more shots at
the cactus. Firing from the hip now, spacing them at
regular intervals. Two misses, another clip on the side
and one placed dead centre to tunnel through the plant
and exit at the rear.

The shot that emptied the gun caused the horse to snort
and attempt to bolt. The hobble prevented this and the
gelding fell hard to his side with a snicker of pain.

Barnaby Gold slid the acridly-smelling Peacemaker
back into the holster and allowed the side of his long black
coat to cover it. Then he eased back the other side of
the coat with his left hand, swivelled the second Colt on
its stud, thumbed the hammer to cock it and squeezed the
trigger that was unguarded at the front.

He did all this slowly and deliberately, his good-
looking face with its embryo moustache as blank as
before. But when the gun belched its bullet, the recoil
hurled him into a half turn. And he showed a scowl of
shock as he almost lost his footing on the shale.

He sucked in some warm morning air and let it out

with a low whistling sound. Glanced down at the eagle-butted gun with his hand still fisted around it, and muttered softly: 'Goddamn it to hell.'

Then vented another spontaneous gust of laughter, like after he had hurled away his hat the first night out from Fairfax.

The gelding seemed to sense the good humour from which the raucous sound was born and ceased to struggle as the man returned to him. The horse lay still on his side and the man was merely grinning as he dropped to his haunches to release the hobble.

'It seems we both have a lot to learn, boy,' Gold said softly to the animal as he took a hold on the bridle to urge him to his feet.

Then he mounted and clucked the horse into movement northward. And, as he rode, he ejected the spent cartridges from both guns and reloaded the chambers with fresh shells from a carton in one of the saddlebags.

The empty cases dropped to the dusty, hard-packed trail and glinted in the sunlight. A mile beyond this, a line of horse droppings provided further evidence that a lone rider had passed this way. And, before he paused at midday to establish his presence with a fire under a mesa wall, two cheroot stubs had been discarded among the gelding's hoofprints.

He fired a dozen shots here, aiming at a projection of rock from the mesa. The horse was disturbed by the reports and the drifting smoke that assaulted his nostrils. But this time he made no attempt to bolt. Barnaby Gold learned to brace himself for the recoil of both guns, although his marksmanship did not improve very much. Only once did he adopt the double-handed grip with which he had killed Coombs and Dwyer. He was as accurate now as he had been then and when he saw this, he made the clicking sound with his tongue.

An hour after setting out from his lunchtime stop-over he reached an intersection of trails marked with a three armed signpost from which the elements had long since eroded the lettering. But he knew from eight years ago, when he and his father had driven the newly purchased hearse from Tucson, what had been printed on the signpost. On the south pointing arm, Standing. West, Tucson. East, Tombstone.

He veered the gelding to the left, to ride him slowly along a broad, shallow-sided valley and thirty minutes later allowed the grateful animal to drink from a narrow and muddy creek that crossed the trail. Then to crop at a patch of grass which grew in a grove of pinyon to the side of the trail. He stayed there for as long as it took him to smoke a cheroot then, as the dust of something moving showed on the trail far to the west, he remounted and clucked the horse across the creek.

The valley was not flat-bottomed and after a few minutes the small dust cloud was lost to his sight beyond a rise: several rises. And almost another half hour was gone from the blistering hot, glaringly bright afternoon before he saw the dust and its cause again. The driver and shotgun of the Tucson-to-Tombstone stage had their first sight of Barnaby Gold.

The Concord was being hauled slowly toward the top of a gentle but long grade, the four-horse team straining to drag their burden over the final few yards to where the trail went between two grotesquely eroded outcrops of sandstone at the crest. The animals knowing from previous scheduled runs along this section of trail that they would soon be at the creek. While the two middle-aged men up on the box seat were relishing the prospect of a short stopover in the shade of the pinyon trees beside the ford. Inside the stage, the three male and one female passengers dozed or peered out of the dusty windows, enjoying the slow progress over the long upgrade that kept the pitching and rolling and jolting to a minimum.

Then the lone rider emerged between the outcrops about fifty feet ahead of the lead horses.

'Hell's bells!' the driver growled, and wrenched on the reins to bring the team to a halt.

This as the shotgun rasped: 'Shit!' and reached among the roof baggage to snatch up his Winchester.

And the passengers vented cries of alarm followed by shouted questions as the sudden stop jerked them out of lethargy.

Barnaby Gold continued to ride the gelding at the same easy pace as before to close the gap with the stalled Concord. Until the shotgun rider was on his feet, a bullet levered into the breech of the repeater which he aimed from the shoulder as he ordered: 'Don't come any closer, mister!'

The young man complied with the command but showed no facial reaction to it: as two elderly heads were thrust from the open windows of the doors on either side of the stage. To gaze, wide-eyed with trepidation, at a tall, thin, entirely black-clad figure seated astride an all black horse. With a double barrel Murcott hanging from one side of his saddle and his long frock coat opened to display one gun on his left hip and another in a holster tied down to his right thigh.

'You make a move to draw, mister, and it'll be the last thing you ever do in this vale of tears,' the man with the aimed Winchester warned.

Gold's hands remained where they were, their heels resting on either side of the saddle horn, fingers loosely clasping the reins.

'You've got me wrong.'

'I got you plumb dead to rights, mister.'

Gold's calm attitude and easy unafraid posture astride

the gelding acted to placate the agitation of the passengers. And intrigued the bearded driver.

'What's the idea?' he asked. 'Ridin' on over the crest that way?'

'Been ridin' the same way all day.'

'But you must've heard the stage rollin' up the hill?'

'Right.'

'Didn't occur to you that you might scare us half to death? Lookin' the way you do and just showin' up between the rocks like you did?'

'No.'

The driver showed exasperation. 'That we might figure you was fixin' to hold us up? And Craig here might plug you?'

'I might still figure that and I might still do it, Jonas.'

'Rubbish!' This from the sour-faced old lady leaning out of a window of the Concord. 'This young man is quite obviously an innocent traveller.'

There was a grunt of approval from the passenger at the same window. The two men on the other side of the stage looked less inclined to agree with her opinion.

'So put away that rifle and let him pass,' the woman snapped. 'And let us get on ourselves. I have no wish to be late arriving at our destination.'

'Jonas?' Craig growled.

'Reckon she's right,' the driver answered, biting on the inside of his cheek as he peered quizzically at the man in the saddle, whose dark-hued appearance was relieved only by the blond hair which showed below each side of his hat brim. 'He looks like death itself with all that black, but it's my belief he's just too dumb to know any better than to do what he done. Let him by.'

Craig was not quite able to mask his relief at being allowed to escape from the standoff situation without need to use the Winchester as more than a threat.

Z

'All right, mister,' he said. 'On your way. But I'm gonna be coverin' you with this here rifle for a time to come.'

Gold said nothing. Clucked to the gelding and steered him to the side of the trail to go round the stalled Concord. The muzzle of the Winchester tracked his slow progress.

'You certainly are something frightening to come upon at first sight, young man,' the woman told him in a grim tone as he rode by the door window from which she leaned.

'We are what we are, lady,' he replied. 'Appreciate you speaking up for me.'

He directed a personable smile toward her and she fluttered her eyelids and got patches of colour in the centres of her cheeks: like a young girl excitedly embarrassed to have attracted the attention of a boy she admires.

'Appreciate this, too!' Jonas called after him. 'Take care when you get to the way station at the head of the valley. Steve Brodie is real suspicious of all strangers. Even ordinary folks.'

Then he yelled at the team and cracked the reins over their backs. And the shotgun, taken by surprise at the suddenness of the restart, cursed as he was forced to sit down hard and almost pitched off the stage.

Barnaby Gold waited until the Concord had gone over the brow of the rise between the outcrops, then paused to take out a cheroot and light it. The remnants of the smile he had shown to the old lady continued to glow in his green eyes and crinkle the skin to either side of them.

He dropped the spent match on the trail.

CHAPTER TEN

HE indulged in a further period of target practise during the late afternoon, just before the gloom of evening encroached along the valley in the wake of the sinking sun. But this time he combined drawing with shooting. And he also parted the seams of the pocket in the left side of his frock coat. So that, with his hand apparently in the pocket, he could swivel the eagle-butted .45 and trigger a shot in secrecy. Though during this training session he fastened back the coat so as not to blast holes through the fabric.

He took care to get the priorities right – did not sacrifice accuracy for speed.

The gelding pricked up his ears and turned his head in response to the first shot fired. But then resumed what he had been doing – flicking his tail at desert flies. While Barnaby Gold continued to blast at a tin can balanced on a dead log over a distance of ten feet – as the beans which had been in the can began to bubble in the small cooking pot on the fire.

He was pleased the gelding had adapted so quickly to

the crackle of gunfire. And not displeased with the progress he was making toward becoming competent with the pair of handguns. It would take time to become what Murchison, the Standing gunsmith, had termed a fast draw quick-fire artist, but he felt it was within his capabilities to achieve this. For he had a feel for the revolvers. A certain indefinable sense of the guns being an extension of himself when they were in his grip. It seemed entirely natural to him to have them in his fists.

It surprised him when he first became aware of the sensation which, strangely, was not accompanied by any feeling of power.

Maybe that would come, unbidden, when he was skilled enough to hit a target the size of the tin can twelve times with twelve shots in twelve seconds. For which he was patiently prepared to wait and see.

He had never rushed at anything in his life except the childhood scrap with the three kids on the icy New York City sidewalk. And marriage to Emily Jane Freemont.

He first saw her on a storm-lashed night filled with lancing rain and streaked with a barrage of fork lightning. On the trail linking Fairfax with Standing.

Barnaby Gold had gone to the larger town to buy some pine wood from the lumber merchant there. And, despite the threat of the impending storm, had taken time out at a back room of the cantina.

The rain was teeming, the wind was raging and the northern sky was jagged with lightning to the accompaniment of thunderclaps when he paid off the madam, climbed on to the seat of the fully laden flatbed wagon borrowed from John Hogg and drove out along the south trail.

Anyone else who drove off on to the open trail on such a night would have been called crazy. But people had grown bored of using the same old worn out terms about

Barnaby Gold Junior, so his departure passed without comment. And only the whore named Maria was sorry he left for, she had heard, men like the son of the undertaker did not often frequent cathouses. Certainly she had never sold herself to anyone like him.

He was no more than a mile out of town, needing to concentrate all his attention and strength on the chore of driving the heavily loaded flatbed – to keep the storm-frightened team on the trail and guard against running the rig into a mud patch where it was likely to sink to its hubs – when he saw the girl. Starkly illuminated in a series of lightning flashes that turned black night into blue day for all of three seconds.

It was obvious she had seen the approaching wagon in an earlier streak of brilliant light for she was halted at the side of the trail, turned sideways on to peer back into the force of the wind-driven rain.

She was about forty feet away then and provided a tableau of wanton beauty. A girl on the verge of womanhood, close to six feet tall and with a high, firm-breasted figure – the wind pressing the sodden fabric of her dress hard against her flesh, contouring its every rise and hollow from ankles to shoulders. And streaming out the long blonde hair from her head so that the classically sculptured features of her oval-shaped face could be seen to be beautiful, even though they lacked the softening effect of the frame of tresses upon which so many not quite so comely women rely. She was no older than eighteen.

She waited, without expression of discomfort or relief, until he had drawn the wagon to a halt. He had to shout to be heard above the hiss of rain, howl of wind and claps of thunder.

'You must be making for Fairfax?'

She held up the large and underfilled carpetbag and he

took it. And she was up on the seat beside him, unaided, by the time he had set down the bag.

'If that's where you're going, Mr Gold, it's fine with me.' She spoke with a New England accent, the tone rather husky.

'How come you know who I am?'

'I was told.'

The burlap-draped freight on the wagon sheltered them from the full force of the wind and he saw that, with her hair – still held in a semblance of ringlets despite being soaked – hanging to her shoulders, she looked very young indeed.

He set the rig rolling, intrigued by her reply but showing no eagerness to learn the details behind it. While the girl sat silently beside him, as unmoved by the weather as he was: both of them maintaining an easy attitude that suggested it was the most normal thing in the world for them – total strangers – to be riding a wagon at night through the full ferocity of an Arizona thunderstorm.

Then the bay horse threw a hindshoe – but good fortune caused this to happen at a point where the trail ran along the base of a bluff pocked with many deep caves.

'We're going to have to hold over here,' he yelled as he angled the team toward an arched opening into the rockface.

The turn placed them into the wind and her hair blew to touch its ends to his face.

She waited until they were in the pitch blackness of the cave and the rig was stopped, the sounds of the storm muted. 'Whatever you say, Mr Gold.'

The cavern was forty feet high and half that distance wide at the entrance. As he steered the team inside, he could not see what lay ahead and relied on the horses to use their equine senses. Until the length of the wagon was in shelter, when he commanded the halt.

Her words echoed faintly.

'I'll rest the horses, then ride the good one to Fairfax and bring another.'

'Good.'

Lightning flashed and the cavern was seen for a second to be higher and wider than its entrance. And deep enough to accept three wagons and their teams in line astern on its sandy floor. But Gold did not move the rig further into the shelter. Climbed down from the seat, and feeling his way in the pitch darkness, unhitched the horses from their traces. Hobbled them close by.

If the girl made any sound, he did not hear it against the storm and the creak of leather, the thud of hooves on sand. But when his chore was done and another lightning flash filled the cavern, he saw she was gone from the wagon seat. Was sitting now, delving into the carpetbag on her lap, on a three foot high, bench-like flat rock against a wall of the cave.

He lit a cheroot and kept the match alight to show himself the way to where she was sitting. And just before the heat of the flame forced him to drop the match, he saw she had found what she was looking for – something made of a delicate fabric which she used as a towel to dry the rain on her face. Then, as he sat down beside her, she started on her hair.

'Bad night for walking.'

'My name's Emily Jane Freemont and my father died a week ago today. But you don't have to worry about that. I'm all cried out. I thought I'd never stop, but I did.'

'In my business, I have reason to know that grief doesn't often go on for long.'

'I was told you were an undertaker.'

'Your father died in Standing?'

'On the stage a day away. The people were very good. They fixed it for him to ride on top with the baggage. So

103

I could fix for him to have a decent burial in a town cemetery.'

She finished drying her hair and laid out the makeshift towel on the rock between them. In the glow when he drew against the cheroot, Gold could see it was an undergarment. A lace-trimmed chemise, white and pink.

'Father was in the newspaper business. He wasn't very lucky. We failed again in Tucson. He heard there was no newspaper in Standing so that's why we came. It was his heart caused him to die.'

She leaned her back against the rock wall and sighed. 'The world can be real cruel sometimes, can't it, Mr Gold?'

'What else do you know about me except for my name and what I work at?'

'That Standing folks like your father more than you. Except for the girls at the cantina.' There was a flash of lightning as she spoke of the Mexican whores and he was able to see her face brilliantly lit. It showed not a sign of repugnance. 'I saw you go in there tonight after the wagon was loaded. While I was eating supper in the restaurant and wondering what I would have to do for the price of my next meal and a roof over my head tomorrow night. Mr Glazer, the sheriff, was also having supper. He told me about you.'

'Because you asked, Emily Jane?'

'Because I asked, Barnaby.'

'Why?'

'Because when I first saw you in Standing I felt the same way about you as you did about me when you saw me on the trail.'

'You don't beat about the bush, Emily Jane.'

'Mr Glazer said that neither do you. When you have anything to say. Which isn't very often.'

There was a long pause, almost as if Barnaby Gold

were giving her an example of the taciturn trait in his nature. And during this minute or so, the sounds of the storm lessened.

Then: 'Any man who saw a girl like you out on the trail on a night like this would have given you a ride.'

'I'm not denying it. And if a ride is all I get from you, I'll be no better or no worse off in Fairfax than I was in Standing. There will be some kind of work I can do there to keep from starving?'

Her tone added the query.

'Sure. I guess so.' He felt tongue-tied for the first time he could remember.

'And since Fairfax is a much smaller town, there will be less men like your fellow undertaker in Standing. Mr Ward. And Mr Grogan, the butcher. Mr Johnstone who has the restaurant.'

There was no lightning flash to illuminate her face now. But her voice did not take on any tone of disgust as she listed the elderly widowers and committed bachelors who had propositioned her.

'Isn't that so?'

'I guess they're all decent enough people in Fairfax,' he answered. 'Enough of them, anyway, to be a good influence on those who might be like Clay Ward and the others you named.'

There was another long silence between them, as Gold finished smoking the cheroot and the wind lessened still further, the thunderclaps fading deep to the south-west.

'I've been known for my candour since I was a small girl in Portland, Maine, Barnaby. But I've never been so forward as this. Now that father is dead, though . . . I can cook and keep a clean house, sew and make smalltalk with other women of all types. Since my mother died giving birth to me, it was necessary for me to do all those things for my father as soon as I was old enough and we

105

started to move about the country.'

'Goddamnit to hell, Emily Jane,' Gold said, and he sounded almost breathless in contrast to the even tone in which she had catalogued her skills.

'But how good I am at doing what the Mexican girls do, I don't know. Because I have never allowed a boy to do more than kiss me on the lips. But I don't think I'm being immodest when I say I know I look to have what men like in that matter.'

Gold rose to his feet. And his voice was almost as husky as that of the girl when he blurted: 'The horses are well rested now. Time for me to ride.'

'Whatever you say.' She spoke without disappointment, petulance or sullenness. Agreeing to the will of another in much the same way as Barnaby Gold would have if their positions had been reversed.

He swung around and strode to where the horses were hobbled. Released the black gelding and led him alongside of the wagon out into the now gently falling rain.

'Be back in a couple of hours!' he called.

'There's nowhere else I can be,' she answered without rancour.

Riding the big black horse bareback through the slackening rain and then under a dimly moonlit sky streaked with grey clouds was no hardship to him. He had never been on a horse until his father brought him out to Arizona, but he had taken to riding with the same ease as he was destined to experience eight years later when he took up the handguns.

He did not hurry on the ride into Fairfax, taking the time to think long and deeply about the beautiful young girl waiting back in the cave. It was still before dawn when he reached town and no one else was awake.

He bedded down John Hogg's horse in the blacksmith's stable and left town again with the team which pulled the

106

hearse. And on the return trip to the cave he maintained the same easy pace as before. But this time it was simply to conserve the strength of the two geldings. There was no more thinking to be done on the subject of Emily Jane.

The round trip had taken the best part of three hours and dawn was on the verge of breaking when he led the horses into the cave, which was beginning to fill with the first grey light of the new day.

Emily Jane seemed not to have moved from the bench-like rock. Showed no sign of having slept. And had certainly done nothing to her hair and face the way most girls would have in similar circumstances.

'You should have got out of those wet clothes for a while,' he said. 'You could catch a bad chill.'

He hitched the horses to a front wheel of the wagon and when she saw him do this she got to her feet, a smile of subdued eagerness lighting her pale blue eyes and parting her full lips over very white teeth.

'They're dry now, Barnaby. But I'll get out of them if you want. And since you didn't harness the animals to the wagon . . . ?'

She let the query-marked sentence hang in the lightening, warming air.

He halted six feet in front of her.

'It would have to be marriage. If we lived in Fairfax. And right now, I couldn't leave and have the responsibility of – '

'Emily Jane Gold . . . ' She looked pensive, then smiled more brightly. 'It has a good sound to it.'

Her high-necked, long-sleeved, ankle-length dress – a lighter shade of grey now that it was dry – had buttons at the back. When she reached to unfasten them, the movement thrust forward her firm, conical breasts. He could feel her eyes watching his face, just a little nervous, as he gazed at her undressing. She wore a chemise as delicately styled as the one which still lay on the rock. And panta-lettes and hose of silk, leather shoes styled for city wear more than trail walking.

She showed no sign of seductiveness as she took off and discarded each item of clothing. Nor shyness, until there was just the knee-length chemise protecting her total nakedness.

'Since this is my first time, Barnaby, I've no idea what I should say now.'

'Since you're not a whore, I'm not sure, either,' he answered, as he took off his topcoat and spread it on the sand between them.

Then he undressed, as artlessly as she had done, but took the time to roll up his jacket and pants to form a pillow.

'I've seen father. We were very frank about such things. I know what to do, but not how . . . Oh, I never saw father like that.'

Barnaby Gold straightened up from pulling off his long-johns. And when she saw the state of his arousal, her com-posure cracked for the first time.

'I'm glad you didn't,' he told her, and stepped across the makeshift bed. To take her in his arms and kiss the lips which were offered to him, her head tilted, her eyes closed.

He felt the twin pressures of her breasts against his chest through the chemise. Her thighs remained pressed together, reluctant to admit his pulsing need. Her arms embraced him, her fingers touching his skin lightly. He reached down the length of her body, caught hold of the hem of the chemise and raised it. She held him more firmly and for a moment he thought she was seeking to prevent him taking off the final garment. But there was attack, not defence, in the way her fingernails began to dig into his back.

He used his superior strength to draw their bodies apart. But their lips remained locked until the chemise was bunched up around her neck.

'Barnaby, Barnaby, please help me to be good. Better than any whore you've ever had.'

He tossed the chemise aside and held her away from him. She tried to press her nakedness to his, but he prevented this, afraid of climaxing before the coupling was complete.

'Easy, Emily Jane,' he said softly, and picked her up in his arms. Where she became totally submissive. Allowing him to stoop and lay her on the coat with her head on the pillow. When she closed her eyes and allowed her thighs to part slightly.

Her skin was pure white and flawless, her nipples and their aureoles pale pink, the triangle of hair at the base of her belly just faintly darker than the blonde on her head, getting lighter and finer in the line that reached up to her navel.

After he had feasted on the sensuous sight of her nakedness for several seconds, she snapped open her eyes and asked: 'Don't I please you, Barnaby?'

'Just do what comes naturally, Emily Jane,' he answered as she smiled upon seeing that his wanting had not diminished.

Then she closed her eyes again, and submitted without even a token struggle to the pressure of his knees splaying open her thighs.

He had never taken a virgin before, so that what happened next was as unexpected by him as by Emily Jane. She was wetter than any whore he had known, and the entry was almost as easy. She cried out in pain rather than pleasure, but just for a second contracted as if seeking to reject his penetration. This was an instinctive reaction – and so were all the others which followed in a frantic period which could have lasted no more than thirty seconds.

The scream became a moan. Her legs parted wider and were raised. Her arms came up from the sides to encircle his back. One hand went to his head to bury his face in her neck as she fastened her open mouth on the flesh of his shoulder. She matched her body movements precisely with his. Her erected nipples were like points of heat on his chest. Her legs encircled him and she locked her ankles together. Her teeth sank into his shoulder, then were torn free by the powerful urge to voice the sounds of passion which rose to her throat. 'Faster, deeper, more, more, more, oh, oh, ooooohhhhh . . .'

She climaxed several seconds ahead of him and her muscles became lax. But as he continued to pound his own wanting into her, it brought her to the brink of new arousal. And at the moment of his draining she was as demanding as ever. So that it required all his lust-diminished strength to break from the locks of her holds around him.

The taking of her maidenhead had spilled a lot of blood, stained both of them. A virgin she undoubtedly had been and, because of his lack of experience with any woman who was not a whore, Barnaby Gold Junior felt no uneasiness as he sprawled out on the sand and she lay on the coat: both of them breathing deeply as they recovered from the frenetic copulation. And she said:

'Barnaby, what have I been missing until now?'

They were married two days later.

The sun was setting, splashing a blood redness across the sky, when he rode to within sight of the stage line way station at the head of the valley. He had seen smoke from a chimney smudging the sky for a mile or so, but did not see the building from which it came until he rode around a stand of pinyon at the edge of a broad plain.

The station was of timber, sited in the trees on a patch of land which had been cleared to provide materials for its construction. There were two buildings, one of them long and low to provide living accommodation for the man who ran the place and a rest room for stage passengers, and the other higher – a stable with hayloft under the peaked roof, out back with a corral at the side and a fenced yard in which some chickens ran.

A man was feeding the fowl as Gold showed on the trail. But when he saw the newcomer he hurled the pail of bran to the ground and ran into the low building. To reappear on the threshold after banging open the door, when the black gelding was reined to a halt on the hard-packed area where countless stages had paused for the teams to be changed.

He was holding a Winchester, the hammer cocked, slantwise across his chest. A short, skinny, almost completely bald man of about sixty with a round, small-eyed face on which any expression other than a scowl would have looked out of place. He was dressed in dungarees and work boots. No shirt.

The glow of a stove fire showed in the room behind him. In the dying rays of the sinking sun, Gold could just make out the lettering on the sign which was nailed above the open doorway. *Huachuca Vista Way Station.*

'This here place only got facilities for stage line passengers, mister,' Steve Brodie said, his high-pitched voice even more unfriendly than his expression and stance.

'I can pay for a bed and food for myself. Stabling and feed for my horse.'

'Stage line pays well enough for me to get by.'

111

Gold clicked his tongue against the roof of his mouth. 'I heard you didn't welcome strangers, Mr Brodie.'

The Winchester was angled away from his body with a fast movement. But did not quite travel far enough to aim at the mounted young man. This as the scowl took a firmer hold on the bristled, dirt-grimed flesh of the older man's face.

'How you know my name?'

'From the man who told me you don't welcome strangers. Driver of the Tombstone-bound stage.'

Brodie looked less uneasy. 'Jonas Turner told it like it is, mister. Strangers is likely to bring trouble as well as anythin' else.' The sun was now gone from the sky and it was obvious Brodie was having to strain with time-weakened eyes to see Gold in detail. 'And appears to me, mister, that you're the kind has trouble for a middle name.'

'Okay, Mr Brodie. Sorry to have held up your evening chores. Bye bye.'

Gold clucked to the gelding and tugged gently on the reins to turn him away from the front of the way station. He sensed the small eyes of the inhospitable man gazing curiously at his back as he rode along the trail for a few yards, then made to angle into the pinyons to the north of the station.

'Hey, where you think you're goin', mister?'

Gold halted the gelding again and glanced back. 'Bed down, Mr Brodie. And the timber seems like a better place than the scrub desert out there.'

He waved a hand to indicate the flatland that stretched away to the north and west in the fast gathering dusk.

'Shit, I ain't havin' that!' Brodie snarled angrily, his temper pitching his voice higher.

'You're not?'

In the two words and the way Barnaby Gold sat casually astride his mount, there was an implicit challenge. No aggressiveness – simply a calm asking of what the man intended to do about the situation. And for long moments Brodie was growing angrier in his predicament. Then: 'Shit, come on back here, you ornery cuss. Best you're where I can see you than skulkin' about in the trees.'

Gold showed his personable grin, which Brodie failed to see, for he turned and went into the building as the newcomer started back along the trail. Lamplight augmented the glow of the stove fire at the window and open door.

'I ain't waitin' on you, mister. You take care of your own animal.'

Gold did this, dismounting and leading the gelding around the side of the low building, along the yard fence and in through a gate to the corral. While he attended to the needs of the horse in the stable where six others were enstalled, he heard Brodie out in the yard, cursing at the chickens who had gorged themselves on the contents of the discarded pail which was supposed to be enough for two days.

He left the saddle and all its accoutrements in the stable and returned to the main building the way he had come – to enter through the front door, removing his hat as he did so. Stepping into a spartanly furnished parlour, most of the furniture crudely made from the same kind of timber that was used in the construction of the building. Except for a large stove in a corner and a good quality, worse for wear rococo-style sofa placed nearby.

Brodie was seated comfortably on the well-padded sofa, chewing on a wad of tobacco. The Winchester was back on brackets in the wall just inside the door. After bawling out the chickens, he had also had the time to set another place at the rough hewn pine table which was attended by four chairs.

'Close the door and make yourself as comfortable as you can here, son. I'm bakin' a beef pie and roastin' some potatoes. You don't like that kinda grub, you'll have to eat outta your saddlebags. You want hard liquor, you're in the wrong place. I'm sworn off it.'

He offered this welcome with reservations after an appraising look at the newcomer, apparently surprised at Gold's youthfulness: visible in the light from the ceiling-hung kerosene lamp now that he had taken off the black Stetson.

'Appreciate it, Mr Brodie. Sounds good.'

Gold took off the frock coat and hung it from one of a row of hooks under the rifle. Then unbuckled his gun-belt and released the tie of the holster from around his right thigh. The man on the sofa showed a sour expression as he watched this.

'Cookin' and takin' care of livestock is what I'm good at, son. Reckon from what I'm seein' I know what your line is.'

'Is there a place I can wash up?'

'Ain't worth me openin' up the passenger facilities just for you.' He jerked a thumb at a door behind the sofa. 'Through there. Five minutes to supper time.'

With the door left open, enough light entered the bedroom for Gold to see the narrow bed, the closet and the washstand with the bowl and pitcher on it. The aromas of cooking food and burning kerosene were not strong enough to mask the stink of body odour emanating from the unmade bed. There was no soap or facecloth, but there was a towel which smelled much the same as the bedclothes. The water in the pitcher was clean.

'I'm an undertaker by trade,' Gold said when he

emerged from the bedroom, the dust of a day on the trail cleansed from his hands and face.

Brodie was carrying the pie to the table, on which a dish of roast potatoes already steamed. He looked at Gold with surprise.

'Sit yourself down and eat, son.' He returned to the stove, raised the lid and spat the mess of chewed tobacco into the fire. Then came back to the table, pulled out a chair across from Gold and cut into the pie. 'Said I weren't gonna wait on you,' he reminded after piling potatoes on to his place alongside the pie.

Gold helped himself to the food.

'Undertakin' explains them black threads you wear, son. But business in your line so slow you gotta go out put folks in need of the service you give?'

Brodie talked with his mouth full. Barnaby Gold waited until he had swallowed a first mouthful of the delicious tasting pie – the beef tender as butter and the pastry thin and light.

'Been told a Texas family will be gunning for me soon, Mr Brodie. The guns are for protection.'

The man across from him nodded. 'I don't wanna hear no more, son. Better than even chance strangers mean trouble. The less I know, the less chance of me gettin' tangled up in it.'

'Barnaby Gold is my name, Mr Brodie.'

'I don't give a shit about that, son.'

'Appreciate it if you'd remember it.'

'What the hell for?'

'Should anyone come by and ask if I was through this way.'

'You mean you want those Texans to catch up with you?'

'I want to go to Europe, Mr Brodie. Prefer not to leave any unfinished business behind.'

'Matter of honour or some such crap?'

'No, sir. Matter of when I leave something behind me, I don't want to have any reason to look back.'

CHAPTER ELEVEN

THE marriage of Barnaby Gold Junior to Emily Jane Freemont was the subject of much talk in Fairfax for a long time after the ceremony: conducted by the Reverend Baxter at the church in front of a congregation comprised of the boy's father, John Hogg and Jack Cater – the blacksmith acting as best man and the barber giving away the bride.

In female circles the gossip was for the most part on the lines of marry in haste and repent at leisure. While the menfolk spoke incredulously of how 'that oddball kid' managed to find and win Emily Jane, who had to be one of the best looking girls in the Territory. But it was envy, rather than some Godgiven vision of the future. That caused so many citizens of Fairfax to predict a bad end to the match.

For twelve months, by which time the subject of the whirlwind courtship and hurried marriage had palled – and it became obvious to the eagle-eyed that Emily Jane's belly was still as flat as ever – the couple lived happily in the parlour, kitchen and two bedroom accommodation attached to the business premises of Barnaby Gold and Son. Sharing this with the older Gold, who when he had taken a little too much to drink in the saloon could be persuaded to say so much and no more about his son and daughter-in-law.

'I never knew there could be another person in the world the same style as my boy. But there surely is and Emily Jane is her name. Keep themselves to themselves in the house the same as out in the town. Like him, she don't say a lot, but she's as respectful as he is. Keeps the place as a new pin and cooks near as well as my Elvira used to. Never did think my boy'd be able to find himself a wife who'd suit his ways. But them two, they're like a hand and a well fitted glove. Only thing is . . . ' And here his voice would trail off and he would shake his head, sadness in his eyes. 'Only thing is, without doing or saying anything, it's like they don't want me to share in this happiness they got. Like they reckon it's in short supply and they don't have any to spare. Real strange. Real strange . . . '

Emily Jane went to Standing on the day before their first wedding anniversary. She knew what present Barnaby was going to give her, for she had seen him working on it. A William and Mary style lowboy in walnut with trumpet turnings and teardrop pulls of brass. While watching him at the carpentry she had seen that his set of wood chisels was the worse for wear. And he was sure that when she set off north along the trail, driving a buckboard borrowed from the Reverend Baxter, that she was intent upon buying him replacement tools.

But Emily Jane did not return to Fairfax until she rode in wrapped with a blanket and slumped over the horse led by Floyd Channon.

When she had not come back by nightfall, Barnaby saddled one of the black geldings and rode for Standing.

118

The mining town was quiet, dark and locked up. But Sheriff Walt Glazer, wrapped up warm against the chill night air in his sheepskin coat, was seated on the buckboard, the horse already in the traces.

'She's gone, boy. On the Tombstone-bound stage that left midday. Bought a five dollar one-way ticket.'

Her purse had held just ten hard-saved dollars.

Barnaby Gold hitched the saddle horse to the rear of the buckboard as the lawman climbed down.

'Appreciate the trouble you took with this,' the young man said to the older as he dropped on to the vacated seat and unwound the reins from around the brake lever.

'Don't you want to know if she left any message for you, boy?'

'She wouldn't.'

Glazer sighed sadly and shifted the pipe from his mouth. 'You're right. Just said to tell the Fairfax preacherman this rig could use some axle grease. I attended to it.'

Gold nodded.

'Sorry, boy.'

'Appreciate the sentiment, Mr Glazer.'

'Seemed to be a spur of the moment decision she took. Fred Grange over at the hardware store . . . he said she was in his place, askin' advice on some carpenter's tools. When the stage was about to pull out. And she just left his store, run to the stage depot, bought the ticket and got aboard. Yelled that thing about the axles needin' greasin' out the window of the stage.'

Barnaby Gold nodded again, and did not look back, along the northbound trail the stage had taken, as he started the buckboard rolling in the opposite direction.

Sheriff Glazer was quick to make it known around Standing that, as far as he could see from the way the boy took the news, he had been halfway expecting something of the sort. And this was the consensus of opinion when word of what had happened reached Fairfax – brought by a group of matrons who had visited the town to the north on a shopping expedition. For all the younger Gold had told his anxious father was that Emily Jane had gone away for a while: and he didn't know when she would be back.

Then tongues began to wag as frantically as at the time of the unexpected marriage. The girl had only pretended to be the same kind as her husband. In truth, she could stand his taciturn reticence no longer after the initial flush of the romance of marriage had faded and she found she was unable to change him. There was little enough social life in Fairfax for a girl like Emily Jane, but maybe he even forbade her to attend the summer picnics, July Fourth celebrations, barn-dances and church get-togethers that he himself shunned. This was the explanation most often agreed on during after-Sunday service discussions sparked off by the women of the town. In Jeb Stone's saloon, provided Barnaby Gold Senior was not present, the menfolk were inclined to leer over a cruder reason for the girl's decision to leave.

'He's tall and he's pretty strong from havin' to dig all them graves. But just 'cause a man's big built don't mean he's got plenty of what a lot of women want.'

And the drunker the men who took part in talk of this nature, the more genuine were their opinions that the young husband had failed his beautiful wife in the marriage bed. For each could recall, aided by liquor-warmed images in their minds, those times when Emily Jane had smiled knowingly at him. As if she had realised how her breasts displayed in profile or the mere movement of her hips when she walked inflamed the desire of the man who looked at her.

Some of the men at these late night drinking sessions in

the saloon even spoke in detail of such incidents. In their stores, out on the streets, even at the Golds' funeral parlour: and reflected regretfully that they had made no advances to discover the extent of Emily Jane's frustration.

But, as before, in time the gossip died a natural death. For no one dared to ask the deserted young husband for his version of what had happened and eventually it had to be accepted that Barnaby Gold Senior was speaking the truth when he said his son had not confided in him. And the boy became the same as before Emily Jane entered his life. Which, it was realised, was little different from while the girl was with him. Except that once again he engaged in his lonely pursuits in entire solitude instead of having Emily Jane at his side.

On long rides through the surrounding hills. Making fine furniture in the workshop when there was no calls for caskets. Reading books and magazines which came to him through mail-order. Being coolly polite to all who greeted him but never inviting conversation.

But he never used Jeb Stone's saloon in Fairfax any more. Or went to Jack Cater's for a haircut. Instead again began to make irregular trips to Standing. Always there was a business reason for the visit. But always, too, he spent time in the Silver Lode Saloon. Even longer in a back room of the cantina. Sometimes had a haircut.

And the name of Emily Jane was never again mentioned within his hearing until the day his father died.

Steve Brodie went to bed early at the Huachuca Vista Way Station – straight after washing up the supper things. Taking care of this himself, maintaining that the chore was necessary whether he was alone or had company so it didn't count as waiting on his guest.

'Sofa's pretty comfortable, son, and if you keep the stove goin' you won't need no blankets. If you ain't here no more when I get up, I won't think none the worse of you. Night to you.'

He had bitten off a small chew of tobacco before starting on the dirty dishes and now spat it into the fire, before going into the bedroom and closing the door behind him.

There had been a great deal of talk as the two of them ate supper, most of it by Brodie about his days as a railroadman in the south before the war brought him west. Barnaby Gold merely agreed or disagreed from time to time, as the man with a reputation for disliking strangers made the most of having an easy listener.

Now, on his own, Gold added some fuel to the fire, pushed in the stove damper and took off his boots. Doused the kerosene lamp and accepted the invitation to make use of the sofa. It was not long enough to lay out flat, but it served well enough with his knees bent double and his frock coat rolled up to form a pillow.

He slept, but not for long. Was roused by the clop of slow-moving hooves out on the trail. Approaching from the east. As he swung his bare feet to the floor, the door from the bedroom opened.

Brodie was naked except for a filthy blanket draped over his shoulders. 'If it's a Texan come for you, you be sure to tell him I ain't no friend of yours, son,' he blurted as he scampered toward the door. But stopped short of it to lift down the Winchester from the wall brackets. Then retreated to his bedroom and left the door ajar.

Enough moonlight filtered in through the dusty window to show Barnaby Gold his way across the room. He was in less of a hurry than Brodie had been and reached the window just as the rider slowed the horse, as if to come to a stop in front of the way station.

The horse was a scrawny-looking grey, weary from a

long time on the trail. The animal quivered with the equine equivalent of a sigh at the prospect of rest. But then the rider glimpsed the face at the window, clearly seen in the moonlight. And the horse was viciously heeled forward again – lunged to the command with a snort. In the instant before this, that rider – a mere dark silhouette against the low hanging moon – had seemed to be petrified by fear. Then leaned along the neck of the horse, head averted, to be carried at a gallop away from the station and in moments was hidden by the timber.

The figure astride the horse was tall and slim, attired in a sombre-hued garment which seemed to be combined of a cape and a hood that billowed with the slipstream of the sudden burst of speed. An ankle showed above a low-sided boot and a hand was raised to hold the hood in place.

'He gone on by?' Brodie called as the hoofbeats receded out across the plain.

'Seems she likes company as well as you do, Mr Brodie.' Gold replied as he returned to the sofa.

'It was a woman? Headin' out over the flats alone at night?'

'Right, Mr Brodie.'

'Well, what do you know about that?'

'Nothing.'

The bedroom door was closed and Gold resumed his relaxed position on the sofa. Waited to fall asleep again and it came soon. Lasted until the rat-tat-tatting of a gila woodpecker at a dawn labour roused him. For a few moments he continued to lay on his back, watching the perceptible increase in light level as dawn broke.

Then something alarmed the woodpecker to flight. And Gold swung his feet to the floor and reached for his boots. For he had heard the same thing as the bird. A voice.

' . . . you men. It's said the old man who runs this

123

place will shoot at anythin' that moves. If he ain't sure what it is.'

The words were spoken in a whisper, but in the stillness of early morning the voice carried. Maybe fifty yards – or more. Down the east trail. Reached the ears of Barnaby Gold clearly enough for him to recognise the speaker as Sheriff Walt Glazer.

'I don't figure the boy to be here, Walt. He's smarter than anyone ever give him credit for.' This was Dan Murchison, the Standing gunsmith from whom Gold had purchased the two Peacemakers.

'Shit, the dumb cluck left a trail a near blind man could follow.' Sam Grogan, the town's butcher, said.

'Didn't I say that's been botherin' me?' Glazer replied. And sounded anxious still.

'What we gonna do, Walt?' a fourth man asked, as sour-voiced as Grogan. It was Slim Wilder who owned the Silver Lode Saloon.

'You men wait here,' the lawman said. 'I'll go check the stable. If that new horse of his is in there, we'll call for the boy to give himself up. If it ain't, then we'll rouse the old timer and have some breakfast before goin' out over the flats.'

There was no sound of the sheriff dismounting. Just of his footfalls, which were carefully measured as he sought to tread lightly.

Expressing no sign of how puzzled he was by the whispered conversation, Barnaby Gold had already made several moves by this time. Aware that the men from Standing would hear any carelessly loud sound he made, he rose from the sofa and with his boots under his arm crossed to the row of pegs by the door. Buckled the gunbelt around his waist, tied down the holster and then donned his frock coat and hat.

The dawn light was still grey and the air was chill: the

leading arc of the sun not yet above the eastern ridges.

He reached the door to Brodie's bedroom just as the gate in the corral fence squeaked when Glazer opened it. And one of the horses in the stable whinnied softly at the approach of a man.

The catch on the door clicked but the hinges operated silently. Brodie slept peacefully, breathing deeply and emanating more foul odours into the bad-smelling room. His Winchester leaned against the wall at the bedhead. The room's only window was in the building's end wall, offering a view of the pinyons and a section of the trail.

Fifty yards had been about right. For it was at this distance that the trio of Standing merchants waited for the sheriff to return. Looking cold and weary, trail-dusty and unshaven. Dividing their nervous attention between the main building of the way station and the higher one across the yard out back.

The first shaft of the new day's sunlight angled low from the east, its intensity dissipated by the trees.

The chickens began to cluck.

Barnaby Gold moved from the threshold toward the bed, boots still held under his left arm, his right hand fisted around the wooden-butted grip of a Peacemaker.

Out on the trail, the three men from Standing were directing all their attention to the stable now.

The corral gate squeaked again.

Steve Brodie grunted, on the brink of awakening.

Walt Glazer's footfalls could be heard.

Gold set down his boots on the floor and remained in a stoop, extending his left hand toward the round, heavily bristled face of the man in the bed. He clamped the hand hard over the mouth and thumbed back the hammer of the .45. Pressed the muzzle to the suddenly violently pulsing temple.

'Good morning, Mr Brodie,' he said softly as the man's

eyes snapped wide open and raked along their sockets to stare in terror at the expressionless face of his captor. 'Looks like it's going to be another nice day. Bad one to die on.'

CHAPTER TWELVE

IT was a similar fine day when Barnaby Gold Senior suffered the heart seizure that killed him.

Mid-afternoon, just an hour after he left Jeb Stone's
saloon where he had played some hands of five card draw
with John Hogg, Jack Cater and Stone. When these men
heard of his passing, they recalled that he had coughed a
great deal during the game. But no more than on many
other occasions when his bronchial condition refused to
respond to the warmth and dryness of the Arizona
climate. And maybe he had not been his usual cheerful
self. Less talkative and slower to smile. Preoccupied with
some problem that he could not relegate to the back of
his mind despite the diversion of the low-stakes card
game in pleasant company.

Certainly he stayed longer in the saloon than was
usual: and drank a good deal more than his normal quota
of the expensive bourbon Jeb Stone stocked specially
for him.

But, since he was known not to enjoy the best of health,

there never was any question raised about the manner of his death.

He entered the carpentry workshop where his son was smoothing down the frame of a Massachusetts-style ladder-back chair, only a vividness of colour in his cheeks revealing that he had taken more than his usual number of drinks. A man in his early sixties, five feet ten inches tall with a paunchy belly and a thick neck. Siver grey hair that added a distinguished look to otherwise nondescript features. Clean shaven and, as always, neatly turned out. Attired in a dark city-style suit complete with vest which had a watch chain hung across the front.

'I'm late, son,' he said.

'There's nothing to do.' The younger Gold continued to rub down the carved wood of the chair which stood on the bench.

'Took a few more drinks than I do usually.'

'It's a hot day.'

The father came into the brightly sunlit room that smelled of sawdust and glue and varnish and paint. 'Ever since you made that shovel handle I knew your skills should be put to better use, Barnaby. Than making boxes to be buried to rot in the ground.'

The young man interrupted his work to join his father in examining the chair, which was a perfect copy of one illustrated in a catalogue. 'Maybe if I had to do this for a living I wouldn't enjoy it so much.'

A nod. 'You should go to Europe one day, son. See all that fine furniture in those mansions and castles and palaces.'

'Intend to.' He began the smoothing process again.

His father watched him but, as at the saloon, his mind was elsewhere. He said suddenly: 'Something you should know.'

'What's that?'

128

'It's been troubling me for some time.'

From the tone of his voice, Barnaby Gold Junior sensed the enormity of the burden his father was carrying and he curtailed his work to turn to look at him.

'About Emily Jane, son.'

Only the younger man's mouthline altered: tightened.

His father looked down at his hands, which always smelled faintly of formaldehyde.

'What about her?'

'The day before she left, you were off somewhere in the hills. I wasn't too well, if you recall. Stayed in bed. She came into my room. To tell me she was thinking of going off, son.'

He looked up at Barnaby Junior, expecting to see some reaction in his face. But there was nothing.

'She cried a lot. Said how she felt buried and useless living here in Fairfax. Was missing the way she was always on the move to new places and meeting new people when her father was alive. How she'd come to look upon me as a substitute father. But had never had the courage to talk to me this way before.'

He paused and this time got what he expected.

'You said she should leave?'

'She asked my advice, son. I told her we only have the one life and if we live it in misery when we can do something about it, it's our own fault. But I said that if she wanted to leave Fairfax, it didn't have to be alone. That, if you wanted, I wouldn't try to talk you out of going with her.'

'She didn't want that, or you would have . . .'

'No, son, she didn't want that.' He gazed down at his hands again. 'Because it wasn't just the town she was bored with.'

He looked up in time to see the nod of understanding. And hurried on: 'Don't take it personal, son. God, that sounds stupid. What I mean is, she said it would be the same with any one man. No matter who he was. She was desperate for new experiences – of every kind. But she felt she owed you a great deal, Barnaby. For taking care of her after her father died. And she was sick with remorse for not realising the way she was then.'

'Walt Glazer said she got on the Tombstone stage by impulse,' the younger Gold put in.

His father nodded. 'I'm sure she did, son. I told her she should think very carefully before doing anything that might cause her more remorse. And when she left town the next morning, I'm sure her mind was not made up. Which surprised me, son.'

He swallowed hard and met the green eyes of the younger man levelly again. Swallowed hard. 'After what happened.'

The mouthline lost some of its tautness now, and the breath was drawn in and expelled quickly. One hand clutched at a leg of the unfinished chair on the bench, as if for support. But the tall, slim frame was held rigidly erect.

'Barnaby?' The colour of drink had left his father's face, which was now pale. Beaded with sweat on the brow and along the top lip.

'It may be best if you leave it to my imagination, sir.'

'Dear God, I have to tell someone, son. All this time I've kept this secret it's been like I'm in a living hell. Sleeping in the next room to you, terrified I might talk in my sleep. Afraid, too, that I might drink too much – enough to loosen my tongue.'

Abruptly, the uncharacteristic tension drained out of the younger man. And he invited, as tears spilled from the eyes of his father: 'Okay, sir. Tell me what happened.'

'She was weeping, Barnaby. Sitting by my bed and holding my hands like I was some kind of anchor keeping her from drifting into insanity. She looked real beautiful.

130

In that white dress with the gingham apron. Her hair done in the bun the way she used to.'

'I can recall what she looked like,' his son said dully. 'In those clothes and her others. Out of them, too.'

'Dear God, son, it just happened. Like neither of us intended it to. She needed comforting and I . . . well, I was just as . . . as troubled as she was. If it hadn't been in the bedroom. With me just in my nightshirt. If she hadn't reminded me so much of your mother that – '

'Don't use her as an excuse,' his son interrupted tersely.

The older man shook his head, so violently the tears on his cheeks sprayed away. 'I don't want to make excuses, Barnaby. I deserve to be loathed and despised by you. But I want you to know why I've been able to ease my conscience just a little over the years since it happened.'

'Why? Isn't it working any more?'

The older man mopped at the beads of sweat and tears with a handkerchief. 'I'm going to die soon, son. In our business we've heard from enough bereaved people to know that it's not unusual for some who are close to death to have premonitions of what's going to happen.'

'I'll take care of the arrangements, sir.' Because of the lack of emotion in the words, they sounded cruelly callous.

His father grimaced his anguish.

'Damnit, boy!' he flared, and a deeper shade of red patched his cheeks. 'Now I'm telling you, I've got no reason to lie to you. I believe it's true that Emily Jane didn't want it to happen, just like me. But when it did happen, she showed herself in her true colours. There's no other way to tell it but crudely. I never got it in her. She tore her clothes off like she was hysterical. She was stark naked and it had been too long for me. Soon as she slid under the bedcovers, it was over for me.'

His voice began to rise and a strange glittering light

131

entered his eyes. And even though he spoke, his mouth held the line of a grimace of disgust. 'Then she really did get hysterical. Panting and sweating like an animal in rut. First she cursed me for doing it before I was inside her. Then she used every trick every whore knows to try to get me interested again. And you know I've got good reason to know about them from that time after your mother died.

'And when that didn't work, because I was feeling sick to my stomach over the whole rotten business, she did it to herself, boy. With my night-time candle. And I did throw up then, Barnaby. While she was sprawled out on the bed at my side, doing that to herself. And telling me she had to do it every night. Sometimes twice. In the day-time when we were out, as well. Even those nights when you and she – '

'That's enough!' his son cut in, his eyes squeezed tight closed as if he could see a vivid image of the event taking place in the workshop.

For a few moments, it seemed that the older man was too deeply enmeshed in the blurting out of his confession to call a halt. But he won the struggle with the inner force which had been driving him. And he looked and sounded totally drained as he said: 'Yes, son, that's enough. Just to say that I eased my conscience with the knowledge that I didn't . . . didn't touch her. And every night since she's been gone – driven off as much by her shame as by the way she is, I'm sure – I've given thanks to God that it was me and not some other man in this town, or in Standing, whom she came to. And after her lust had been satisfied, she was ashamed, son. Deeply ashamed. Begged me to help her. But all I could tell her was to see a doctor. Not that I'd ever heard of any remedy for what ailed her.

'That's it, Barnaby. Like I say, you're probably going

132

to hate me for as long as I have to live. But I won't mind that, now you know it wasn't anything to do with you that Emily Jane took off. And I beg of you not to hate her. Because she's sick, son. She can't help the way she is.'

He started to cough. Just a clearing of the throat at first. But it rapidly took a hold of him, and its effect went deeper – reaching down to its cause in his lungs.

His son opened his eyes and stood silently watching as the older man's body spasmed, his face going purple and the veins standing out like cords under his skin.

The younger Gold lifted the chair off the bench, still held in a one-handed grip. Then he took hold of another leg and thrust the chair above his head.

His father stared at him with eyes that were filled with the tears of agony. He reached out with both hands, palms toward the chair-toting figure, fingers splayed in a tacit gesture of defence.

'No, Barnaby!' he pleaded between wracking coughs.

Then he moaned, and withdrew both hands to clasp at his chest. His face was suddenly contorted into an ugly mask as a bolt of pain shot through him.

His son began to crash the chair downward.

The father dropped to his knees, mouth gaping to its widest extent, but venting no sound. The eyes became glazed with the film of death.

The son continued the down path of the chair, but swung from the waist. So that the skilfully crafted timber smashed against the edge of the bench. The back snapped from the seat. He raised and brought down what remained. The frame broke off. Another blow and the stretchers came away from the legs. But he was not satisfied until he had picked up the back and smashed the slats from the supports.

He remained expressionless as he committed the act of wanton destruction. And was just as unemotional when he checked that his father was dead, tossed the remains of the chair on to a heap of discarded waste timber and only then left the workshop. To go along the street in search of Doctor Trask to ask for a death certificate.

Since he was never to give the matter any thought, he was never to know if, had his father not suffered the heart seizure, it would have been the man or the bench against which he smashed the chair.

'Barnaby Gold! This is Sheriff Glazer of Standing! I know you're inside! And I'm orderin' you to come on out with your hands up! Have a sworn-in posse of deputies along with me!'

While Steve Brodie was held still and silent by the pressure of a hand over his mouth and a gun muzzle against his temple, the black-clad young man watched through the bedroom window while the quartet from Standing were positioned to the orders of Glazer.

Grogan in the trees to the east, Murchison sent to the rear and Wilder and the lawman moving across in front of the way station. Glazer announced his presence out front, which probably meant the saloon owner was in the cover of the trees to the west. All the men had drawn revolvers from under their overcoats before moving to their designated positions.

'Any sound from you before I'm through and you're dead, Mr Brodie,' Gold warned levelly as he released his grip on the man and sat down on the bed to pull on his boots.

The foul-smelling old timer swallowed hard and shifted his eyes to look at the rifle leaning against the wall.

'Thoughts I don't mind,' Gold said. 'It's words and deeds you have to beware of.' He stood up, his boots on, and raised his voice: 'I hear you, Mr Glazer! I'm coming out! To find out what you're talking about!'

'Hey, Walt! He's got the oldster with him!'

This from Sam Grogan who was able to see into the sunlit bedroom as Brodie rose naked from his bed at a gesture from Gold.

'Don't anybody do anythin'!' the lawman yelled anxiously. 'We got plenty of time to talk.'

'Ain't you gonna let me get dressed, mister?' Brodie asked.

'They're all men out there. And the sun's up.'

The old timer glowered defiantly at Gold, dragged a blanket off the bed and folded it, skirt-fashion, around his waist. Then complied with another gesture of the .45 and shuffled out of the bedroom. Gold was close behind him, not aiming the gun until they were at the door which opened on to the trail. When he rested the barrel on the scrawny, naked shoulder: angled so that the muzzle was in line with the underside of the man's jaw.

'Appreciate it if you would open the door, Mr Brodie.'

'But what if that sheriff starts shootin' soon as – '

'Walt Glazer never shot at anything except quail in all his life.'

'And what if I won't?' he countered, his voice not quite attaining the tone of reckless defiance he intended to express.

Barnaby Gold made a clicking sound with his tongue against the roof of his mouth. 'In the past two days I've killed four men, Mr Brodie.'

'Jesus.'

He hurriedly lifted the latch and pulled open the door with one hand while the other continued to hold the blanket up around his waist.

Walt Glazer stood in the centre of the hoofprinted and wheel-rutted area where the stage teams were changed. Despite the warmth of the newly risen sun he

135

was hunched in his sheepskin coat, the collar turned up to brush the underside of his hat-brim at the sides and back. He was holding his revolver, low at his thigh and aimed down at the ground. He stared hard at the opened doorway, the frown on his fleshy face becoming more firmly set when he saw the threatening .45 resting on the shoulder of the almost naked old timer.

'I figured you'd do as I told you, son,' he growled through teeth clenched to the stem of the pipe that angled from a side of his mouth. 'My guess is you had cause for the killin'. What the courts call extenuatin' circumstances. You're bein' stupid now.'

'Appreciate it, Mr Glazer, if you'd have Mr Murchison, Sam Grogan and Slim Wilder come join you. It would make Mr Brodie here happier, too. Less chance of him getting his face blown off by accident. If they did something behind my back I might misconstrue.'

'Gold, you're bein' real – '

'Just do as I say, Sheriff. And have Mr Murchison saddle my horse and bring it out front here.'

'Please, mister, do it!' Brodie begged. 'If he's really killed four guys already, he ain't gonna care about one more, is he?'

Surprise became mixed with the grimness on Glazer's face. But he suppressed the impulse to demand an explanation. Did not shift his attention away from the two men in the doorway when he raised his voice to yell: 'Slim, Sam! Come over here! Dan, go to the stable and saddle his horse! Bring it out front! And no heroics! There's a man with his life on the line here!'

Grogan cursed, but there was otherwise no vocal response to Glazer's orders. The tall and thin Wilder appeared first, then the stockily built Standing butcher. Both were resentful of the situation and obviously blamed the lawman for mishandling the attempted arrest.

'Toss your guns out on the trail.'

They did so.

'You killed four men?' Glazer posed.

'Guess the one you know about is Floyd Channon, Sheriff?'

Although Glazer was on the Standing town payroll, Fairfax made a contribution and was included within his jurisdiction. The lawman and the two temporary deputies flanking him showed their puzzlement. But only Brodie was aware of a reaction from Gold, as he felt an increase in pressure of the Peacemaker barrel on his shoulder.

'It's not a name I know. We're here to take you in for the murder of Clay Ward.'

Barnaby Gold made the clicking sound and murmured: 'Goddamnit to hell.'

CHAPTER THIRTEEN

'WHEN'S the next stage scheduled through, Mr Brodie?'

'What?'

'He asked the time of the next stage,' Glazer growled.

'Westbound. One o'clock this afternoon.'

'That's good.'

'You know somethin', son, I think you're innocent. But that ain't gonna make any difference to what you plan to do, is it?'

'Right, Mr Glazer.'

When the elderly Dan Murchison appeared with the black gelding saddled and the bedroll lashed to the animal, he was obviously relieved to be instructed by the lawman to toss his gun out on to the trail with the others. And he was equally compliant with the politely worded instructions that Barnaby Gold gave him. To go out back to the stable again, fetch some rope and cut it into lengths and bind the wrists of Glazer, Grogan and Wilder behind their backs.

Grogan cursed, Wilder smouldered with silent rage and Glazer continued to give his reasons for believing the

young man innocent of the killing of the Standing undertaker. When these three were securely bound, Gold moved
Brodie off the threshold of the way station and had him
tie Dan Murchison in a similar manner. But first allowed
him to use a length of the rope to form a belt for the
blanket. Then he holstered the .45 and bound the wrists
of Brodie.

'Be back in a while,' he said, swung up into his saddle
and rode the rested, fed and watered gelding along the
east trail. Found where the Standing men had left their
horses, made a string of them and returned to the way
station. Reached there as Grogan was trying to curse
Wilder into standing back-to-back so they could untie
each other's bonds. 'In time, you'll do it,' he told the
glowering butcher evenly.

'And have to take the one o'clock stage because
you're takin' our horses?' Glazer countered dully.

'Unless you can talk Mr Brodie into loaning you the
exchange team in the stable, Sheriff.'

Only the lawman showed he had already thought of
this, by his lack of reaction.

'Whichever, we'll find you, kid!' Grogan snarled. 'And
it won't matter a shit whether you're innocent or guilty of
knifin' Clay Ward. Horse thieves get hung, too.'

'He isn't exactly stealing them, Sam,' Murchison said
placatingly.

'Takin' them without the owners' permission,' Glazer
put in, revealing a trace of suppressed anger for the first
time. 'Amounts to the same thing.'

'Bye bye,' Barnaby Gold said, and clucked his gelding
forward, still clutching the reins of the lead horse in the
string.

'And good friggin' riddance,' Steve Brodie growled
sourly. 'Strangers is almost always trouble. I've always
said it.'

Gazing after the departing black-clad rider, Walt Glazer ruminated: 'And they don't come much stranger than that one.'

CHAPTER FOURTEEN

SHE had run the scrawny grey gelding into the ground some five miles to the west of the Huachuca Vista way station. Winded him into agonised exhaustion and left him to his fate where he had collapsed at the side of the trail on the bank of an arroyo. The dusty ground on which he lay was thick with signs to show how he had struggled without success to get to his feet. The white lather of sweat, crusted by the cold of the night desert air, indicated the extent to which she had driven him in her terror after seeing the face at the way station window.

There was a baleful look in his deep brown eyes when he raised his neck and turned his head to look at the dismounting Barnaby Gold. As if he blamed any passing human being for the ill-treatment he had received at the hands of one of them. His diminished strength did not allow him to keep his head turned and his neck raised for long. And he lay flat out on his side again when the man reached him, slid the Peacemaker from the holster.

'Maybe if she hadn't seen me back there, boy,' he said quietly in a soothing tone: as he stooped to stroke the

animal's matted coat along his neck. Simply to have something to say. To comfort the gelding in his final moments
before the big .45 cracked out and drilled a bullet into his
head from point-blank range.

His own gelding did not even prick his ears to the
explosion which sounded louder than it was in the desert
stillness. The other four horses were made uneasy by the
report.

Then Gold studied the ground beyond the area of dust
disturbed by the struggles of the horse. And saw that she
had taken the obvious route – continued on foot along
the trail west. Frightened still by the face at the moonlit
window and of the barren wilderness to either side.

He lit the first cheroot of the day before remounting
and setting off in her wake. And before he was many yards
away, the first of several buzzards soaring high against the
unblemished blue of the sky had swooped from a speck
to a discernible shape to take a closer look at the fresh
carcase.

One saddlebag and a canteen had been held fast under-
neath the doomed gelding but cut leather showed she
had taken their mates. So hunger and thirst would be no
problem to her for awhile. Just the cold of the night and
the heat of the day – and the fear in her mind.

He rode at a measured, easy pace through the morning
and into the afternoon. Unskilled at tracking, he made no
attempt to hunt for difficult to see signs of her passing.
Did see where she had relieved herself and, nearby, two
screwed up candy wrappers.

Then spotted her, far ahead on the fringe of the
shimmering heat haze, a few minutes after he had started
to direct occasional glances over his shoulder: seeking a
first sight of the westbound stage.

He asked for a trot from his gelding and the string of
horses at his back matched the increased pace. Anything

more would have been too much to demand of these animals, which had been ridden all night from Standing to the way station.

She saw him and the horses emerge into clarity from the heat shimmer and lunged into a run, dropping her burdens from terror. But then realised escape was impossible and stopped, turned around and retraced her steps. Was sitting on the ground between the saddlebags and the hooded cape, drinking from the canteen, when he halted the string of horses in front of her.

There was no fear in her bruised face or posture now. Just sad resignation to whatever he had in mind for her.

'Barnaby, I thought you would be well on your way to Europe.'

'Not yet, Maria,' he told the whore who had failed to please Clay Ward.

CHAPTER FIFTEEN

SHERIFF Walt Glazer had told Barnaby Gold as the men at the way station were being tied up: 'It was Maria from the cantina found him, son. In his bedroom with a knife stickin' out of his back. Sprawled out on the floor near the hole under the boards where he stashed his money.

'He was still alive. Just. Accordin' to the woman. Seems she was payin' Clay a regular nightly visit when you showed up to dicker a price on the hearse. And he told her to take a walk and come back later. She heard you and him cussin' each other on account of you wanted more than he was willin' to pay.'

'Maria didn't like goin' with Clay. So she stayed clear of him a long time. But after a while she got curious about why he wasn't down at the cantina raising' hell because she hadn't come back.

'So she went back to his place on Silver Mine Road and found him like I said. He had enough life left in him to tell her you'd stuck the knife in him, son. Then cleaned out his cache. Two thousand four hundred and six dollars and ninety cents.

'Rang true, that part. Be just like Clay Ward to recall exactly how much he had to the cent in the last seconds of his life.'

The sullen Steve Brodie had made no mention to Glazer of the woman who had ridden by the way station in the pre-dawn hours.

Now it was Maria talking, as dull-voiced as the sheriff had been, while she rode the lead horse in the string behind Gold as they headed back eastward along the trail.

'Barnaby, you heard – perhaps saw – some of what he was doing to me. He was an evil man.'

'He was no saint, Maria.'

'Nor me. I am a whore and must expect to be humiliated and sometimes hurt by the men I go with. But I have no wish to be a whore for the rest of my life.'

'You're through with it now.' He arced the stub of the cheroot away as the Tucson-bound stage showed on the trail ahead.

'I heard you talking with *Señor* Clay Ward, Barnaby. When you agree to take what he offers, I look through the window. It is well known in Standing that he has much money hidden at his place. After you have gone, I go in to steal his money. But he finds me. And I used the knife on him. This is the way it happened, Barnaby. But I will tell it differently to Sheriff Walt Glazer.'

'You say whatever you like to him, Maria. Long as it's not what you told him the first time.'

'Barnaby, I waited long time before I tell the lies. Until after you are gone. To Europe, I think. Then I tell him. And leave the town while the sheriff is getting together the other men to come after you. I do not know but I think that if they do not find you and come back to town – find me gone – they might guess I lie. That it was really me who killed him. But by then, I will be far away. Not to Europe, but far away.'

'Sure, Maria.'

The stage was much closer now, moving no faster than the two riders and the three riderless horses behind them.

'Barnaby, do not think too badly of me. We had some good times together, yes?'

'You provided a service, Maria. And I paid for it.'

He unhooked the Murcott from where it was hung on the saddle and rode with the twin barrels of the shotgun resting across the horn. When there was just a hundred yards between the gelding and the lead pair of the Concord's team, he thumbed back the safety catch to free the internal hammers.

The driver said something to the shotgun rider, who pumped the action of the Winchester resting across his thighs. Both men looked hard at Barnaby Gold but said nothing. Four faces peered out of the windows on the passing side. Initial trepidation altered to intrigued curiosity on the faces of four men passengers and the crew up on the seat as the stage and the string of five horses passed without any vocal exchange. And it was obvious that everyone aboard the Concord knew of the events at the Huachuca Vista way station earlier in the day. But all the passengers were unknown to Gold.

The team in the traces were reasonably fresh – had shared stable space with the black gelding during the night. Which meant the men from Standing had had to be content with the animals that had hauled the stage from Tombstone to the way station.

Neither the young men nor the whore astride the horses said anything until after the dust from the Concord's

146

passing had settled on their clothing and sweat-tacky flesh.

Then: 'Barnaby?'

'What?'

'You think they will hang me?'

'I don't know.'

'I am a woman.'

'That I do know.'

She displayed emotion for the first time. Said angrily: 'And you do not care?'

'It's not the time nor the place and I don't have the inclination, Maria.'

'Damn you! I mean you don't care if they hang me!'

'There are a lot more whores in a lot more brothels, Maria.'

'*Madre de Dios*, I hate you!'

He made no response and she fell into an angry silence. Could not maintain such a high emotion for long during the glaring heat of afternoon, and became sullen.

They reached the spot where he had put down the gelding. Many buzzards had been attracted to the carcase after the first bird swooped down. All that was left was the skeleton with, here and there, shreds of skin clinging to the bones.

'It was not hard to kill him in town. I could not bring myself to put that miserable creature out of its agony. I hope he did not take long to die.'

Barnaby Gold said nothing in reply to her sad-toned excuse.

She had emptied her own canteen at the time she submitted to capture, but occasionally drank from those hung on the saddle of the Standing man's horse. Then, as soon as the sun was down and the warm evening was on the brink of becoming cold night, she donned her hooded cape.

The moon was up, hard and glittering and casting long shadows, when the pinyon stand with the way station in it showed up ahead. Smoke rose from its chimney.

'We are going to stop here to eat and rest, Barnaby?'

'Mr Brodie wouldn't like that, Maria.'

She made a sound of disgust. 'I think you have become the kind of *hombre* who cares nothing for what others like. If you want it.'

He held his silence. Unhooked the Murcott again as he started across the front of the way station. The lamp in the parlour had been doused at the sound of hooves on the trail, but he could see Brodie's head and shoulders in silhouette against the stove's glow at the window.

'That's right, you cold hearted sonofabitch! You just keep ridin' on by here!'

'Shoot him! Shoot him!' Maria yelled. 'There is much money I can share with you!'

'I got nothin' against whores!' the scrawny man at the window called sourly. 'But twice I got a bad dose of the clap off Mex whores!' Then he vented a mirthless laugh. 'But I reckon that's better than what you give that guy over to Standin'!'

'All *hombres* are bastards!' Maria hissed venomously.

Then they were beyond the way station. With Brodie still yelling at them. Something about the Standing posse being happy about it if he had cause to blast both Gold and the woman into eternity.

But moments later the voice faded from earshot and the clop of hooves on the moon-whitened trail provided the only sounds to invade the riders' private thoughts, as they skirted the vast tract of desert plain and started down the valley through the Huachuca Mountains.

'Barnaby, I am sorry.'

'Save it for the judge, Maria.'

'I mean for calling out what I did to the man back there. But I have no wish to hang.'

'I can understand that.'

'You will tell them how easily I gave myself up to you?'

'Sure.'

They reached the intersection of the trails and it was not until then that the whore made another attempt to gain the sympathy of the silent man riding ahead of her.

'That sign, Barnaby. The way one piece of wood sticks out from another. It looks almost like *el patibulo*. How you say it, the . . .'

'Gallows, Maria.'

She gasped. 'Let me go, Barnaby. You can tell them you found me, but I escaped. You have the money I took. If you set me free here, I could go to Tombstone. You could say I went the other way. Or not say anything at all. Because you could take the money to Europe.'

He tugged on the reins to head his horse and the trailing string down the trail toward Standing.

'Barnaby, *por favor!*' There was a sob of desperation in her voice. 'That man who does not like you back there. From what he said about what I did to Clay Ward, it is certain Sheriff Walt Glazer knows I am guilty. There will be no more looking for you. It is me they will be searching for.'

'Sure, I heard him say that.'

She began to shed tears now, at the lack of emotion in his voice and the relentless way he kept his back to her as he continued to ride toward Standing. 'Then why Barnaby? Why you take me back to face *el patibulo*? You are free to go where you wish. You cared little or nothing for Clay Ward.' She paused in her tearful listing, frantically searching her mind for other items to add weight to her argument. 'If having the money troubles you, you can send it through the mail.'

149

'And there's the horses. Some think I've stolen them.'

'Then leave them with the man at the place in the trees, Barnaby. Surely he will see . . . '

Now he turned to look back at her and she abruptly curtailed her pleas: fear of the utter coldness of his expression driving her into silence. And he was totally unmoved by the sight of her, a pathetically helpless creature hunched in the saddle with large teardrops coursing down her bruised cheeks.

'Personal reasons, lady.'

'I do not understand,' she said, fear of his quiet anger forcing her voice into a whisper.

'It doesn't matter.' He faced front again and after a few moments of listening to her cry, he offered: 'I'll give you a chance, if you want?'

'Yes. Yes, Barnaby. *Si, por favor.*'

'You're not tied to that saddle. You can get off the horse and run.'

She was abruptly suspicious. 'You will allow this?'

'I'm only just learning to handle guns, Maria. You want to be free and I need the practise.'

'*Bastardo!*' she hissed.

'Sure, Maria. And I guess I always will be. Toward women who screw me. The wrong way.'

CHAPTER SIXTEEN

IT was still dark when they rode off the trail and on to Main Street, Standing. Just one lamp was alight in the whole town: this dimly, behind the window in the façade of the law office.

Sheriff Walt Glazer was awakened by the clop of approaching hooves and he was up from the chair behind his desk and at the open door of the office when Barnaby Gold halted the string of horses outside.

The lawman, warm from a glowing stove and his sheep-skin coat, looked to be very well rested in contrast to the weariness of the two cold-pinched riders.

'Good morning, Mr Glazer.'

The older man took the pipe from his mouth to growl: 'For me it surely is, son. For both of you, it ain't.'

'You going to be serious about the horse theft charge?'

He ran a jaundiced eye over the four mounts Gold had confiscated at the way station. 'They look to be in pretty good shape, son. No sweat on that score. You want to get down off that horse and step inside to the cell, Maria?'

'I do not want to hang, Sheriff.'

'That won't happen, girl. Not with a man like Clay Ward the victim. You still got the money that was stole?'

'*He* has it!' She made the pronoun sound like an obscenity.

Gold untied from his saddle the bag the whore had cut from her own. And tossed it to Glazer. 'It's all there, down to the last ninety cents.'

The sheriff caught the bag and nodded. Spared a short-lived smile for Maria. Who was encouraged by this to get painfully down from the horse. 'We can work out somethin', girl. Maybe get you off with a couple of years in the territorial prison.'

'I think I could perhaps sleep for the whole of those two years, *Señor* Glazer.'

He gestured for her to go into the law office. Then, to Gold: 'You can get down from there, son. But don't do anythin' else.'

The black-clad young man did dismount, just as the first grey light of the false dawn made inroads against the darkness of night.

In back of the law office, an iron door was opened and closed. As the key was turned in the lock, the whore sank on to a cot with a sigh of relief. A drawer was opened, the saddlebag thudded inside and the drawer was slid closed again.

The dimly lit lamp was doused. Then a match was struck and the smell of burning tobacco emanated from the open doorway. Glazer appeared on the threshold again.

'I thought you'd given up tobacco, Sheriff?'

'I did. But what with all the hassle I've been havin' . . . Hell, son, time's goin' by. I plan to give you two choices, both for your own good.'

Gold said nothing. Simply eyed the elderly sheriff quizzically.

'You brought her in. Dan Murchison and me maintained that if you found her, that's what you'd do. Sam Grogan and Slim Wilder, they figured otherwise. Take off with her and have a high time on the money that was stole. Then for a while after we got back here and I heard from a Fairfax feller about you blowin' a man to pieces with that shotgun . . . well, I was inclined to share the view of Sam and Slim.'

Night and the stars were gone from the sky now. Just the moon showed pale white in the dawn. Barnaby Gold had taken out a cheroot and lit it. Now stood with his left hand in the pocket of the frock coat. Right one holding the bridle of his gelding. Cheroot angled from a side of his mouth.

'You're going to be more serious about the murder of Floyd Channon than me taking the horses, Mr Glazer?'

'Your choice, son. It was Jack Cater, the barber over to Fairfax, who told me about it. All about it. Now I can arrest you for that killin' and keep you safe in a cell until the trial. And since you killed him for killin' Emily Jane, I figure you'll be deemed innocent. So you'll be turned loose. After which, you'll be on your own.'

'The way I like to be, Mr Glazer.'

'Don't we all know it, son. And that's the other choice I'm offerin' you. To take off the way you intended before this business of Clay Ward and the whore came up.'

'And you'll forget about the other three killings Steve Brodie mentioned?'

A shake of the head. 'I ain't overlookin' them son. All I heard is talk. That old buzzard at the way station spoke of them. And Jack Cater told me there's evidence on the south trail that three men went missin'. Only other thing I know on that score is that three hard types passed through Standin', headin' south, the night before you come here to sell Clay Ward the hearse. I got flyers on

153

them in the office. Wanted for cattle rustlin' up Cheyenne way. Just fifty dollars apiece. They caused no trouble here and Cheyenne is too far. I ain't got no evidence they got murdered.' He took the pipe from his mouth to add: 'I think it best you take off, son.'

'Appreciate it, Mr Glazer. But I'd like to take the time to wash up, shave, eat and rest. And my horse has been ridden a lot of hours.'

. The sheriff was knocking glowing ash from his pipe bowl, grimacing as if the taste of the tobacco was bad after so long off the habit. The leading arc of the sun inched above the ridges to the south-east.

'Shit, son. You always have been too full of cockiness for your own good. And I guess you remind me of the way I used to be at about your age. But this time is likely to be the last time.

'I was real puzzled about the way you was leavin' such an easy trail to follow while me and Dan and Sam and Slim was after you. And it wasn't until after I talked with Jack Cater I found out why. When he told me about the Channon family not bein' the kind to let you get away with killin' one of them.'

He gazed hard into Gold's face and drew no response. Anger rose within him.

'Damnit, why beat about the bush. There's a man named Arkin bedded down in a room at the Silver Lode. Hails from San Antonio. One of a whole bunch hired by the Channons to search for the one you buried over to Fairfax.

'Arkin's like you in one way. He don't say a lot. But he told Slim Wilder enough. Seems the dead man's Pa has an idea his boy's passed on. Him bein' gone away so long. So Arkin and the others just ain't ordinary men. They're pro gunslingers, son. Hired to take care of things if it turns out Floyd Channon is dead and didn't die from natural causes.'

Barnaby Gold clicked his tongue against the roof of his mouth. Said: 'Fairfax folks aren't like Arkin and me, Mr Glazer?'

'Right boy. Same as Slim Wilder who was feelin' pretty damn mean toward you after what you done to us at the way station. Seems the Channons have a lot of money and Arkin and his kind have got some of it to cover expenses. He bought what he knows at Fairfax. Could probably have got Slim to talk for free.'

'Appreciate it, Mr Glazer.'

'Then show it, son. This ain't a gunfighter's town. Clay Ward is the first man ever known to die in Standin' from somethin' other than lack of breath. But it's not just that I want to keep trouble away from here. Like I said at the start, it's for your own good. That twin gunned rig you bought off Sam might make you feel ten feet tall. But up against a pro like Arkin, you might just as well be ten feet wide.'

'Sure, Mr Glazer.'

He made to turn toward his horse.

The batwings of the Silver Lode were pushed open and began to flap.

A Texan drawled: 'Hey, undertaker!'

CHAPTER SEVENTEEN

THE law office was on the east side of Main Street, casting its morning shadow over the two men and five horses standing in front of it.

The saloon was diagonally across the street, its façade in sunshine.

'The dischargin' of firearms inside city limits is forbidden by a local ordinance, you men!' Walt Glazer called thickly, sounding pompous and afraid.

'It'll just be me who'll be breaking it, lawman,' Arkin answered evenly as Barnaby Gold turned slowly around to face him.

He was in his mid-thirties. Perhaps three inches taller than six feet. Thin as a beanpole with a face to match. Ratlike in the manner of Dwyer's features. Dressed in black, like Barnaby Gold. But more stylishly. Boots, pants, shirt, vest, kerchief and Stetson. All the clothing as clean as his freshly shaved face. The bullets in the loops of his gunbelt gleamed brighter in the sunlight than the windows of the saloon at his back. In the holster tied down to his right thigh was a .44 Smith and Wesson hinged-frame Russian revolver with a polished wooden grip. The metal of the gun was recently oiled.

He walked with long but slow strides toward the law office. Loose-limbed. He was in the process of rolling a cigarette, the tobacco already in the paper. He used both hands. Never took his gimlet, light coloured eyes off Gold.

'Anyways, he don't seem to be a man. Just a kid. Shot-gunned Floyd Channon, which I can see happening. Have my doubts about him drilling those other three. Green kid like him.'

'Luck of the draw, Mr Arkin.'

The Texan halted, fifteen feet away from Gold. Pushed the tip of his tongue between thin lips, ready to run it along the gummed edge of the cigarette paper. But first he showed small, yellow teeth in a sardonic grin.

'Reckon it took all the luck due to you, undertaker. Which leaves you fresh out.'

Beyond the opening and flapping closed of the bat-wings, there had been no loud sounds to signal the con-frontation. But the rising of the sun had performed one of its daily functions in rousing many of the townspeople. And those who lived on Main Street in the vicinity of the law office and the saloon had been drawn to windows by the even voiced exchange. Some of whom announced their presence with gasps when Arkin said after gumming the cigarette together: 'Going to light this smoke. Soon as I drop the match, I'm going to draw.'

'I've warned you, stranger!' Glazer snarled.

Arkin had the cigarette in his mouth. Now he took a match with his right hand from a shirt pocket. Held it in front of his face, ready to strike on the thumbnail.

'If you've got an iron under that coat, lawman, best you don't try to get it. Or you'll be as dead as the undertaker before he hits the street.' He struck the match. 'Ready, undertaker?'

Barnaby Gold draped the right side of his coat back behind the holster with the .45 in it. 'If you're through talking, Mr Arkin.'

'I am. Anything you got to say? Before this match burns my fingers?'

'Bye bye.'

He had thumbed back the hammer of the concealed Peacemaker in unison with the striking of the match. Then swivelled it on its stud while the gimlet eyes were concerned with the movement of the younger man's right hand.

Now he squeezed the unguarded trigger.

'Shit!' Walt Glazer rasped.

Arkin threw away the match with a grimace of pain as the flame touched his fingertips. Snarled: 'Jesus, you sneaky –'

His right hand was streaking in a blur of speed toward the butt of the holstered Russian. But the bullet in his belly slowed his reflexes as the blood from its entry wound seeped through the hole in his shirt and ran over his belt buckle. Then the pain hit him and the expression of angry surprise was displaced by one of agony. Which became his death mask when a second bullet blasted another hole in the frock coat. To rise on a slightly steeper trajectory than the first. Drilled into Arkin's chest, left of centre.

The dead man was rigid when he started to topple backwards. Then went limp so that he was twisted up, not measuring his full length in the street under the billowing dust of the impact.

Barnaby Gold's black gelding remained immobile while the other horses made sounds and movements of unease. This as the man responsible for the two shots turned to his mount, taking his left hand from his pocket to steady the bedroll while he pulled the three-piece shovel from its centre.

He could see Walt Glazer staring at him incredulously – and sense unseen eyes watching him in a similar way – as he began to screw the pieces together.

'He was wrong, Mr Glazer. Had some luck left. Slim Wilder forgot to tell him about the kind of gunbelt Mr Murchison sold me.'

'What you doin' now?' the sheriff asked in a voice that was still husky.

'Bury him.' Barnaby Gold displayed his personable smile that lit the green eyes and showed the even teeth. Acted to negate some of the weariness in his heavily-bristled face. 'You'll recall Standing doesn't have an undertaker anymore.'

Glazer struggled to keep his voice at its normal tone. 'If I was you, son, I wouldn't waste the time. Soon as it's known what happened here this mornin', open season's goin' to be declared on you. And all them pro gunslingers that are goin' to be doin' the huntin' will know the kinda irons you're packin'. On both sides.'

Barnaby Gold, the shovel canted to one shoulder, moved over to Arkin, stooped and caught hold of the dead man's shirt collar. Then began to drag him away, in the direction of Silver Mine Road and Clay Ward's funeral parlour.

'You're crazy, son!' Glazer called after him. 'Your luck's run out. So you better start runnin' and keep on with it.'

'Appreciate the advice, sir. But I figure I'd be out of breath long before I reached Europe.'

THE END

NEL BESTSELLERS

T 51277	'THE NUMBER OF THE BEAST'	Robert Heinlein	£2.25
T 51382	FAIR WARNING	Simpson & Burger	£1.75
T 50246	TOP OF THE HILL	Irwin Shaw	£1.95
T 46443	FALSE FLAGS	Noel Hynd	£1.25
T 49272	THE CELLAR	Richard Laymen	£1.25
T 45692	THE BLACK HOLE	Alan Dean Foster	95p
T 49817	MEMORIES OF ANOTHER DAY	Harold Robbins	£1.95
T 53231	THE DARK	James Herbert	£1.50
T 45528	THE STAND	Stephen King	£1.75
T 50203	IN THE TEETH OF THE EVIDENCE	Dorothy L. Sayers	£1.25
T 50777	STRANGER IN A STRANGE LAND	Robert Heinlein	£1.75
T 50807	79 PARK AVENUE	Harold Robbins	£1.75
T 51722	DUNE	Frank Herbert	£1.75
T 50149	THE INHERITORS	Harold Robbins	£1.75
T 49620	RICH MAN, POOR MAN	Irwin Shaw	£1.60
T 46710	EDGE 36: TOWN ON TRIAL	George G. Gilman	£1.00
T 51552	DEVIL'S GUARD	Robert Elford	£1.50
T 53296	THE RATS	James Herbert	£1.50
T 50874	CARRIE	Stephen King	£1.50
T 43245	THE FOG	James Herbert	£1.50
T 52575	THE MIXED BLESSING	Helen Van Slyke	£1.75
T 38629	THIN AIR	Simpson & Burger	95p
T 38602	THE APOCALYPSE	Jeffrey Konvitz	95p
T 46796	NOVEMBER MAN	Bill Granger	£1.25

NEL P.O. BOX 11, FALMOUTH TR10 9EN, CORNWALL

Postage charge:

U.K. Customers. Please allow 40p for the first book, 18p for the second book, 13p for each additional book ordered, to a maximum charge of £1.49, in addition to cover price.

B.F.P.O. & Eire. Please allow 40p for the first book, 18p for the second book, 13p per copy for the next 7 books, thereafter 7p per book, in addition to cover price.

Overseas Customers. Please allow 60p for the first book plus 18p per copy for each additional book, in addition to cover price.

Please send cheque or postal order (no currency).

Name ....

Address ....

....

Title ....

While every effort is made to keep prices steady, it is sometimes necessary to increase prices at short notice. New English Library reserve the right to show on covers and charge new retail prices which may differ from those advertised in the text or elsewhere.(6)